DEFENDING HIPPOTIGRIS

an

Interstellar Alliance

novella

T. L. Smith

Defending Hippotigris

Cover Design by T. L. Smith
Cover Art contributing artist/photographers:
Spectral-Design/Getty Images
Shmeljov/Getty Images
Icholakov/Getty Images

ISBN-13: 978-1494455804

ISBN-10: 1494455803

Acknowledgements

There are so many people to acknowledge, I have to keep it simple.

A huge thanks goes to my mother, Patsy, who never discouraged me from going after whatever I wanted, even if secretly she thought I was crazy for wanting to be a writer. And yes, Chuck, I am writing at 3am.

Another thanks to the rest of my family and friends, who cheer me on as I stumble over each hurdle. The kids-Denita, Adam, Devion, Jayden and Kullen. Rick and Brenda, my movie night buddies, and my brother Bill, who introduced me to Science Fiction.

A special thanks to all my writing friends, particularly Gini Koch, the Wyked Women Who Write and Dr. Bruce Davis, for helping me learn to do my craft better and who make Cons a blast. And my dear friend Sandra Bowen. Love our editing sessions over long lunches, or is that the other way around?

And always, I have to thank the readers who want to share in my insanity. Read on!

Want more from T. L. Smith?

Check out her other books.

Scent of Treachery - an Interstellar Alliance novella
Jayda Maldonado exiled herself from humanity, but even a distant space station isn't far enough to escape the attention of a charming freighter captain and a conspiracy that can kill everyone aboard.

The Thing Down the Road
Be wary of road-side freak shows. You may not like what you find.

Or visit her at:

http://www.tlsmithbooks.com

CHAPTER ONE

U.N. Space Alliance – 2198 CE

Remy leaned closer. "Are you all right, Shara?" He whispered in my ear, though it was more of a shout over the noise in the bar. The official reunion was several days away, but we'd come in early for the week of bar-hopping and 'remember when' tales.

"You look bothered." He stroked my leg. "Lizzy's stories never irked you before?"

I laid my head back on his arm to gaze into his big brown eyes. His long eyelashes still got my heart beating when he fluttered them at me. "I don't know, just tired. Think anyone would mind if we left?"

There they went, flutter-flutter, thump-thump. A smile glistened against his creamy latte skin. "We're on leave." His lips brushed against my ear and out came his Euro-Spanish accent. "I can show you more R&R."

His hand slipped up the inside of my thigh and I grabbed his wrist.

"Lizzy!" She had her audience enraptured with another story, making it twice as hard to get her attention. Remy made it even more impossible. I couldn't pull his hand away without being obvious, and I was beginning to not want to. "LIZZY!"

"WHAT!" From the wicked glint in her eyes she heard me the first time.

Remy slid out of the booth and pulled me with him. "Sorry to break up the party, but Shara's just off temporary duty and she's fighting jetlag. You'll excuse her?"

"Jetlag. Right..." Lizzy wagged her finger at us. "Girlfriend, if I just came home to a stud like Remy, I'd jump his bones too. You know, Remy, Shara and I shared everything growing up. Did she ever tell you about sophomore year at ASU?"

My face turned all the hotter. That was a story I hadn't shared and I couldn't get Remy out of the bar fast enough, followed by cat calls before the doors closed.

Remy looked back through the window as Lizzy threw him an obscene gesture. "She sells children's books with a mouth like that, and what about ASU?"

I refused to look inside, knowing all too well what Lizzy was capable of. "I'm beginning to wonder how we stayed best friends."

Remy swung his head around to look at me. "Wow! Seriously? You two have been attached at the hip since first grade." He tightened his arm around my shoulders. "I'm beginning to worry about you. All these TDYs are taking a toll. You've been… distracted… and something else I can't put my finger on."

"Give me a few days and I'll be fine." Being a head shorter than Remy, I was able to huddle into his side as a cold evening breeze blew.

Framed between the buildings of downtown Colorado Springs, was a nearly full moon. With the brilliance of its glow, I could see a spider web of lights from our home, the

Peary Moon Base. The first solid accomplishment of the U.N. Space Alliance.

Odd, how we'd been there long enough to think of it as home, though I spent half my time traveling. A shiver ran through me. "I'm tired and cold."

"Well, I'll take care of cold first." Remy grinned down at me. He tugged me into the hotel's entrance and across the tiny lobby to the elevators.

Though we'd stayed here often over the years, I couldn't resist looking around. The hotel boasted late 22nd century amenities, but they'd tried to recapture the old-world elegance of early 20th century art-deco. Bronze-hued mirrors, gold streaked black marble and red mahogany wood paneling covered every surface, adding warmth to the lobby the holographic fireplace failed to accomplish. Even the elevator's walls reflected back that finely aged comfort as the doors opened.

For a few seconds I admired the craftsmanship, until Remy whipped me into his arms and kissed me. After his escapade in the bar, I eagerly wrapped my legs around his waist. Thankfully the elevator was modern and the height of the building modest, otherwise we might have given security more to see before the fake-ancient bell announced our floor.

I clung to Remy as he carried me the few doors down to our room. A couple steps past the door, he leaned me against the wall to rip my shirt open. His kisses were hard and deep, and from the feel of his hips grinding against me, I wanted the rest of him doing the same. Remy carried me the last few steps to our bed and dropped me onto it. In seconds he had my boots and pants off, then his.

He kept his promise. I wasn't cold anymore, not with my body curled so perfectly against him. His leg wrapped over mine and his arms held me tight. I loved the warmth of his breath against the back of my neck. This is what I missed so desperately on TDY, feeling this total serenity.

I snuggled deeper into the downy cocoon of our bed. Sleep had been difficult since I got back. Tonight I'd reached that state where ordinary things made me edgy. But Remy fixed that problem too. I felt myself drifting off, though memories still played in my head.

This TDY left me so tired I'd been tempted to cancel our class reunion, but Remy insisted we come. Twenty years. We might not get the chance for another one. Time had changed everyone more than I thought it would.

Some people I didn't recognize at all, but Lizzy reminded us what a wild bunch we'd been. Always in some kind of trouble, usually at her hands. Remy laughed as hard as the other spouses, while new boyfriends were shocked at the vivid details Lizzy disclosed.

I laughed along with them, until her stories shifted to our childhood, particularly her rendition of a second-grade escapade. She'd turned many of our adolescent experiences into children's books. She usually didn't stray too far from the truth, until now. This time she said we ran away because my dad got rid of my dog.

We didn't run away and I didn't have a dog. We did go camping. Her brother had a secret fort in the woods, down the hill from my house. It sat up the bank from the river. At least it seemed like a river to us, fifteen-feet wide and waist deep.

The fort was the boys' place to hang out. Girls weren't allowed. Lizzy and I commandeered it while the boys were at summer camp. Tom-boys both of us, we had no problem camping out, eating the military rations her brother got from my dad, or getting up the next morning to go fishing.

We took the cane-poles and climbed into their little boat, casting off into the river. What we didn't remember were the oars. I thought I could pull us back to shore, but after several days of rain, the deeper river swallowed me. Lizzy managed to help me back into the boat, just before the current pulled us downstream.

The further we drifted away from the fort, the less familiar and darker the woods got. To a couple of seven-year-old girls, we envisioned ending up in China. It wasn't long before we alternated between crying and screaming for help.

Then the river bent around a curve and dumped us into the town lake. We'd have gotten over the embarrassment of not really being lost, except half the town was there. They had a search party out to find us, since we hadn't told anyone where we went.

But why did Lizzy add the dog? Or that we ran away? Why did she change the story? A stab of pain crushed into my temples. Fire raged in my head as hands grabbed me, shaking me. My uncle's face appeared. *"Where have you been? What were you thinking? Your dad is crazy trying to find you. How could you do this after your mother..."*

No, it wasn't Uncle Jimmy shaking me, yelling at me. "Wake up, Shara! Wake up!" Another face came into focus. "What's wrong? Come out of it."

"Remy?" I could barely get my eyes open. My head pounded. Where was I? Our hotel. Colorado. "My head. Something's wrong."

"I can see that. Hang on. I'll get your meds." He rushed to the bathroom, returning with the hypo and a wet towel. "These migraines are getting worse. You need to go back to the doctor." He pressed the hypo into my shoulder and held the dripping towel against my face.

It took a couple minutes before the imaginary hands ripping my head from my body eased up. I curled up, blocking everything out as I pressed my face into the towel.

He pulled the heavy blanket around me as chills replaced the cramped muscles in my body. “Any better?” I could barely nod. “Okay, a couple more minutes.”

His promise was good. Finally, I was able to breathe. “That’s not how I like to wake up.”

“Me neither.” Remy gave me a half-smile. “Surprised the police aren’t knocking down the door the way you were screaming. That’s not normal, and with the dose I gave you, you should be asleep.” He swiped stray strands of hair out of my face. “The way you were irritated with Lizzy, I should have known something was off. Why didn’t you tell me you had a headache coming on?”

“I didn’t feel it brewing. As for Lizzy, I’m not used to her changing her stories.”

“What changes? They were the same stories I’ve heard a dozen times.”

“No they weren’t.” I could see the incredulity on his face. “We didn’t run away and I never had a dog… a dog named...” A surge of pain swelled in my head again. “It didn’t happen that way.” Images flashed in my head of a huge dog with grey and black striped fur. “Zebra…”

Saying the name set off another explosion in my head.

CHAPTER TWO

I'd given up trying to tell anyone I was awake. No one could hear me, not the doctors or nurses, not even Remy when they pushed him out of the room.

I tried to make them hear me, to make him stay with me. Instead Remy and Lizzy leaned against the room's window, staring in at me. I could see they were worried. Hell, Remy even hugged Lizzy.

Something was definitely wrong. I had a headache, no… two headaches. Remy thought I was crazy because I said I never had a dog… but Lizzy talked about a dog named Zebra. The image of stripes flashed through my head and alarms sounded in my ears, followed by a whirling sensation that washed through my whole body.

It didn't take many rounds of 'dog-Zebra-alarms and whoosh' to realize cause and effect, ending with drugs. The dog's name was Zebra. What an incredibly stupid name for a dog. Zebra must have been real, but why couldn't I remember? But I was remembering. A grey and black striped dog, weird looking, all skinny and long-legged.

Whoosh.

Why was Remy still on the other side of the window? I wanted him with me. I was home again. I needed him. I didn't need him on TDY. Then I was a biologist… no…

yes, an astrobiologist? No? Things scrambled in my head. Was I a biologist? Really? It sounded too simple. Of course it did. I really worked as a… a… Whoosh.

Hmmm, there was a word for it, but I couldn't remember what it was. Just like I couldn't remember Zebra.

Suddenly I remembered and tears welled up in my eyes. Dad sent him to my uncle's farm because he kept getting out of the yard. He ate things dogs shouldn't eat. He got aggressive when people got too close to me. Dad was afraid he'd get killed and break my heart, but that happened anyway. A horse kicked him in the head and he was dead. "Zebra!"

Alarms blared and I couldn't see Remy and Lizzy anymore, not through clenched eyes. I tried to cover my ears, but nothing stopped the noise, or the pain. "Mrs. Batista…" Hands grabbed at my shoulders, holding me down. "Hit her with another pulse, 10 eps."

"Doctor, she's not anesthetized."

"10 eps." The hands gripped me harder. "Now, or I'll get someone else."

Almost as soon as she said it, I felt something tighten around my head, my scalp tingled, then burned, and something surged down into my brain. It flowed into my whole body, as if I'd picked up an electrical wire, paralyzing me.

I wanted to scream, but nothing worked. For an eternity it pulsed through me, but as it faded away, so did the pain.

"Mrs. Batista. Can you hear me?" I opened my eyes and rolled them towards the voice. A woman stood over me, a lot younger than me.

"Yes…" My voice came out a whisper.

She smiled. "Good. I'm glad you're reactive this time. I'm Dr. Parsons."

I shifted my eyes to the window. Remy leaned against the glass, but looked relieved. "What's wrong with me?"

"We're still trying to figure that out. You were brought in last night in seizures. Your husband said you experienced a terrible migraine and some memory loss." The doctor touched my shoulder, drawing my attention back to her. "Do you remember any of this?"

"The headaches. I never had them like that before. Is there something wrong? A stroke or aneurysm?" I didn't want to leap that far, but fear matched the pain.

"Not according to scans." Dr. Parsons gave me what she must have thought was a reassuring smile, but I could see the upturned corners of her lips were forced. "I need to examine you. Then I'll let your family in for a few minutes."

"Okay." As weak as I felt, I tried to focus on her, flexing my fingers and toes on command. I described my headaches. "I guess they've been getting more severe. My doctor prescribed a pain killer that seemed effective, until last night. As far as setting it off…" I hesitated again, bracing myself. "It was a story about… my dog… Zebra."

I felt a twinge, but also a tingle around my head. I wanted to reach up to feel what wrapped around my scalp.

Dr. Parsons moved over to the computer, watching the waves on her screen alter. "Hmmm, so far so good. The scans say you were awake before, though unresponsive. What were you experiencing? Were you thinking about this dog when your headache hit?"

"Yeah, I was. I couldn't remember him, then the headaches started, but I remember him now and it doesn't hurt."

The doctor turned and looked at me, frowning. "I'm afraid that's not accurate. We have you hooked up to a Cerebral Impulse Regulator. This last attack let us tune the

CIR, so now it delivers electrical impulses as soon as it recognizes a seizure." She leaned on the railing of my bed. "We have to figure out why they're happening. Can you tell me, when you were on TDY, were you involved in an accident or anything traumatic?"

"No, it was just the usual TDY. I do DNA tests at our colonies…" My head tingled harder. The doctor spun back to her computer screen. "I'm only a biolog… owwww." The pain spiked higher, as did the tingling. "Make it stop!"

"The computer indicates you're blocking your responses." The doctor looked at me harder. "What happened? I can't treat you if I don't know."

"I'm not lying. Nothing happened. I just look for DNA... DAMN!" This time I tried to reach for my head, but my arms jerked up short by restraints. Not just my arms, my legs, my chest. "What the hell…" More spikes, alarms and the thing on my head burned. "Let me out of these!" I twisted my arms harder and one broke loose.

Before I could free my other hand, the doctor was on me, trying to force my arm back into the restraint. I tossed her off me, but someone else pushed me back onto the bed. I took a swing, realizing just before my fist hit, it was Remy.

He took the blow, but looked down at me stunned, his eyebrows scrunched nearly together in the center, though one arched higher than the other. "Shara, it's me!"

"Make them stop!" I clawed at his chest, the impulse to fight trying to surge out again. "Get this thing off me. Get me out of here. Please!"

"No!" He leaned on me harder. "Something's wrong and we're not leaving until we know what it is." He stared me down, eye-to-eye. "If you keep fighting, I'll approve chemical restraints." Married or not, he was using his officer-voice.

His cheekbone already glowed red and his eye puffed up. I'd hit him hard. I stopped fighting. "Make them stop, please." Surrendering took some of the pressure off my head and I collapsed back into the bed.

Remy went to the doctor, helping her off the floor. "I'm sorry, Dr. Parsons. Shara's not a violent person, really."

The young doctor's face turned pink as Remy gushed over her, no doubt batting his eyelashes at her, however innocently. "No, no, I'm more to blame. Disoriented patients sometimes lash out."

Still gripping his arm for support, she came back to stand beside me, transferring her grip to the rails. "You can't remove the headgear. The CIR is hardwired into your brain. Tearing it off will cause permanent brain damage."

I listened to Dr. Parsons, but watched as Remy picked up the restraint I'd ripped my arm out of. He held it open, staring at me hard. No attempt to seduce me into compliance.

She sighed in relief as I laid my arm back into the restraint and let him close it tight, shortening the lead. "I promise, when we get this resolved, I'll take the CIR off."

"I'm sorry I hurt you."

"I've been hit harder. It's a hazard in the ED." Her smile faded. "Now, back to what triggered this. I asked if something happened on TDY and you said no, but the readings indicate otherwise. Think of the CIR as a type of lie detector."

She saw me tense and held her hand up between us. "I'm not calling you a liar; I'm saying something happened you can't remember. Our scans don't indicate any recent injuries, but something was traumatic enough to cause this."

She looked up at Remy. "Have you gotten hold of her commander yet?"

"I left several messages, but I'll try again."

He started to pull his hand from mine, but I clutched it tighter. "Don't leave me."

Dr. Parsons leaned closer. "I have to run more tests. Since your friend's story triggered this maybe she can help." She glanced to where Lizzy stood on the other side of the window. "I want to map the extent of memory loss."

Now Remy switched on his seduction side, giving me his 'you want to do what I want' smile. "She knows things I don't, like ASU." He waved Lizzy into the room.

This was a sucky way to spend my leave. Remy went off with his phone, while Lizzy went with me to the Neurology Lab.

Hooked up to an even bigger scanner and more drugs, I listened to Lizzy tell stories of our childhood exploits. My job was to tap the sensor under my hand if the story deviated from what I remembered.

Lizzy was a great story teller. She made a fortune at it, but it wasn't long before my whole arm trembled from tapping at the sensor. Last night I'd asked why she changed the story, but now I knew I'd forgotten more than one detail. I'd forgotten pieces of us, of me.

I turned my head to the glass-enclosed room Dr. Parsons sat inside. She looked as unhappy as I felt. "Thank you, Lizzy." She forced another fake smile. "I wasn't aware you were Dizzi Lizzi. My daughter loves your books. So Shara, I guess you're Darin' Sharan."

"You're not sounding much the fan." Lizzy smiled slyly.

"I want my daughter free-spirited, but I'd also like her to make it to high school." Dr. Parsons' smile remained fixed. "Plus, she'd freak out if she found out either of you were here, particularly you, Mrs. Batista. She wants to be you. No offense… Lizzy."

“De nada. I hear it all the time.” Her wicked smile only got bigger. “I wouldn’t count on the adventures getting any better by high school.”

“Gee, thanks.” Dr. Parsons looked down at her control panels. “Well, Mrs. Batista. I’m sure you’re ready to move on, so let’s get back to questions. She barely paused to take a breath or let me focus. “You’re not really just a biologist, are you?”

“Of course I…am.” My finger pressed the sensor.

“What happened on your last mission?”

“Nothi…ng!” My fingers twitched on the sensor. I tried to jerk my hand away, but the restraints limited my reflexes. “Nothing happened!” My head thumped along with my hand.

“Okay, clearly something did, something major. Not knowing the real facts, we’ll see what your husband comes back with. Then we’ll see what’s…”

“Shara… Doctor, get in here, now! Shara, don’t…” Lizzy stood over me, her voice lost as again something violently ripped my head apart. I couldn’t even scream this time.

CHAPTER THREE

"Venden zapatos para los angelitos. Que andan descalzos. Duermete nino, Duermete nino..." I knew it was Lizzy. She couldn't sing. The song was bittersweet. Lizzy's mom sang it to me often after my mother died, again after my father joined her. *"Duermete nino, Arru..."*

She stopped singing and called out for Remy, but then I heard a muffled mumbling.

I managed to open my eyes, expecting Dr. Parsons or the nurses, or Remy, but instead I was surrounded by strangers. Beyond them a man held Lizzy, one hand over her mouth.

"No! Let her go!" I squirmed in my bed, but restraints still held me down.

"Sir, she's awake!"

A man leaned over me. "Great, but keep her restrained." His eyes followed mine. Lizzy went limp in the soldier's arms. "We won't hurt your friend."

That second Remy walked in, tapping at his comm. "Lizzy, it works better if you answer." He looked up to see men around me and Lizzy crumpled like a ragdoll. "What the hell...?" Remy was grabbed and gagged, before he could put up a fight.

The man over me waved his arms. “Can anyone lock a damned door?” He rolled his eyes before focusing on me again. “Colonel Kazan!”

Why was he calling me colonel… or by my maiden name?

“We’ll figure this out, Kazan.” Maybe he read my confusion. He glanced at Remy out of the corner of his eye. “Right now you probably prefer Batista.”

He knew who I was and from the smirk on his face, something I didn’t. Something I was forgetting? “I guess it was luck we were coming back to reactivate you.” He lifted his hand where I could see a hypodermic gun. It stung as he hit my neck.

There it was again. Whoosh. He walked over to Remy and held the hypogun between them, speaking low. I couldn’t hear but Remy’s eyes looked lethal, but he nodded and the man put the hypogun away. It was the last thing I saw.

⌘ ⌘ ⌘

I stretched, then remembered being drugged. I also realized I could move my arms. I could move everything. Nothing was attached to my head. I felt around, just to be sure. Untethered, I twisted my legs over the edge of the bed and got to my feet.

I was a little wobbly, but got my bearings by the time I reached the door. Locked. I thumped on the door. “Okay, whoever’s out there, I’m awake.” I thumped harder. “Hello… you brought me here, not the other way around.”

“Col. Kazan, have a seat.” A calm voice spoke from the speaker by the door. “Someone will be right in to answer your questions.”

“Batista. Not even close to a major yet, let alone colonel.” I stalked away from the door. There had to be some kind of mistake, the ranks, and the names.

I didn't sit down, but paced. Who do they think I am? Why would they abduct me from a hospital? I stopped mid-step. My head didn't hurt anymore. Apparently they got something right, but I had to be sure.

"Zebra." Nothing. "Zebra, Zebra, Zebra." I suppressed laughing at what my wardens probably thought.

By my third circle around the room, the man from the hospital walked in. He smirked, just like he had before. "How do you feel, Col. Kazan?"

"Better, but Kazan is my maiden name, and I'm not a colonel." I held my place across the room from him. "Why'd you bring me here? Where are Remy and Lizzy? You better not have hurt them." Threatening sounded odd coming from my mouth, but I meant it.

He sighed, as if annoyed, taking a few more steps in my direction. I circled away from him. "Col. Kazan. I command you bring out your primary."

"You command me? My primary? Seriously?" I started to laugh, but a wave of dizziness hit me. Images flooded into my thoughts, strange images, strange places, and I was there. No, it wasn't me. I staggered backwards into the edge of a table. I clutched it, holding tight. *It is me, no it's not... Oh...yeah!*

"Col. Shara Kazan. I command you bring out your primary."

"I got it! Hang on…" I clung to the table as all the images were replaced by one. In my head a coin flipped over and over, one side Shara Batista, the other Shara Kazan. It landed on Kazan and fingers gripped it tight.

With a long exhale I stood up. "Col. Schaeffer. What the hell is going on?" All the memories of the last week were available to me. Batista was my public life, and Kazan my secret life. "Remy and Lizzy? You sucked them into this? Are you insane?"

"We couldn't wait any longer. I'm fairly sure you didn't want them cracking your skull open. As for your companions, they wouldn't let you go without a ruckus." Schaeffer opened the door, stepping out of the way. "They'll be taken care of until this is done."

"When what is done, exactly?" I grabbed a robe off the foot of the bed. "Do you have my gear? Can't work in a hospital gown."

Schaeffer followed me out of the room. "In your quarters. Once you're settled we'll do a briefing. About 1700 hrs."

"What was wrong with me, the headaches and memory loss?"

"The conditioning didn't stick. A conflict sprang up between instructions to forget the mission and your long-term memory. Hospital records note it was stories of Zebra that triggered it." He let out his breath with his usual level of annoyance. "Apparently one overlapped the other, so when we blocked your TDY memories, we blocked that damned dog too."

He gave me a snide look. "Another day or two and you've have broken through, unless they start cutting."

"Yeah, that wouldn't be good." Flashes of Batista's memories hit me, the dog, running away and half a dozen other memories while he was part of my life. This time they didn't come with seizures.

No headaches either. I let out a breath I wasn't aware I'd been holding. "Were you still at Perry? You said something about coming back for me."

"Restocking, but yes, we're reactivating you. We're getting odd behavior on LR-442. The natives aren't happy you left."

I glanced up at Schaeffer. Normally friends, we hadn't agreed on this one subject. "You've changed your mind?"

Schaeffer remained stolid. "My opinion is still open. You need to return to Hippotigris."

"I just got back. Three month TDYs, that's the deal. I can't be away from Remy…" In my head the coin spun again. I was her again, no I wasn't. The coin landed back on Kazan. "God damn it!" I grabbed at the wall for support. "Zebra, zebr…" My head hurt. "There's still something wrong."

Schaeffer stepped in front of me, his hand gently wrapped around my arm. "The doctor says there's no serious damage done, but you might still trigger on those memories, depending on which of you is up front. We tried to switch her off, but apparently you're no longer a candidate for conditioning. That means you need to fully integrate."

He could see my confusion. "Until you're stabilized, you'll probably swing between your two alters."

"That's just great!"

"It could be worse." His concern hinted of emotion under the staid demeanor. "No telling what they might have done to you, given another hour or two."

I shivered with the thought. They'd shoved wires into my brain, shocking me out of the seizures. "Wait, no conditioning? How's that going to affect my assignment?"

"Don't know yet." Schaeffer's hand slid down to mine and drew it over his arm, easing me away from the wall to continue our walk to my quarters.

CHAPTER FOUR

Schaeffer helped me to my quarters. I was tired again, so I didn't ask any more questions. They could wait until the briefing.

The door to my room slid open, but I froze one step inside. "Remy. You're here!"

"Shara, you're all right?" Instantly he went defensive as Schaeffer followed me into the room. "I cooperated! Now, what's going on?"

I stepped between the two men, glaring back at Schaeffer. This was him being the ass again, not warning me. I looked to Remy, putting my hand on his chest, but the dizziness rushed over me again.

Batista wanted out, but I held tight to the coin. This was going to get worse when Remy found out I wasn't a hostage. Schaeffer planned this, probably to force integration. "I need to explain this to my husband."

Schaeffer didn't try to hide his sarcastic grin. "As you see fit, Col. Kazan."

"You haven't left me a choice."

Schaeffer nodded, but I waited until the door closed. In my head I clamped my hand tighter around that coin.

Remy searched my eyes. "What's going on? Why did they bring us here, and why does he keep calling you Col. Kazan?" He pulled me over to the bed and made me sit down. "Why did they take you out of the hospital? What about your migraines?"

He had so many questions. I wasn't sure where to start. "We need to talk, and you're not going to like this."

His face paled. "You're not all right." He wrapped his arms around me.

His arms felt good, but odd also. He kissed me and it felt wrong. That coin in my hand took on a life of its own, trying to flip over to her. She fought to get out and I was suddenly overwhelmed with a possessiveness I'd never imagined. No! I had him first. I was the one to fall in love with him. I was the one he married.

I was the one who made the choice he knew nothing about. Guilt replaced my sense of ownership. I allowed them to split my consciousness.

A secret couldn't be revealed if it wasn't remembered. Kazan kept the secret when I was Batista, his wife. Batista couldn't remember anything but that other life. But that lie was over. Kazan was my real personality.

Guilt won and I pushed Remy away. "Stop, please. It's not what you think. I'm not sick." I got up from the bed. Remy's eyebrows did that thing they did when he was worried, scrunching together.

"I am Col. Shara Kazan, co-commander of an elite exploration team, a secret division of the U.N. Space Alliance. I've been a member for the last fifteen years, almost from the day I enlisted."

I was trying to hurry, to keep him from interrupting until I got my secret out. "When I married you, I had to make concessions to stay in the Corps. Secrets are too hard to keep, so I agreed to let them split my identities. Here I'm

Col. Kazan. When I get back from my missions, I undergo a process to block my memories, so I can be Capt. Shara Batista. She has no idea I exist. When she goes TDY, I'm reactivated."

Remy's eyebrows only became more welded together.

"I'm the primary, the original."

I could see him thinking behind those brown eyes. "You've been doing this the whole time we were together? Ten years?"

His question surprised me. "You… believe what I just told you, no questions about drugs, brain damage, delusions?"

"I knew something was wrong, something I couldn't figure out. I told you that before things got crazy." Remy took a deep breath, letting it out slowly. "Back to my question."

"Ahhhmm, I agreed to it before we got married." I could see he didn't care for my answer. "It worked, until this glitch. They figured out what was wrong, but now I'm needed back on the job."

"What?" There went the eyebrows again, his lips getting tight. "Just like that? What job? Where? What about me, us? They didn't just kidnap me. They have Lizzy too. What are we supposed to do, forget this hap…pened?"

He never was slow. Another reason I had to split my personalities.

"Are you serious?" He took a step towards me, but stopped at an arm's distance, his hands clenched in anger. "You're going to make us forget this? It's more than just us. People at the hospital will ask questions. Your friends will wonder where you went, where Lizzy is."

We were expected at our reunion and anywhere Lizzy went drew attention, as would her disappearance. No doubt Schaeffer came up with a cover story everyone would believe, but should I say that, to him? No! Not with him glaring down at me like he didn't recognize me at all. I felt hurt.

But I shouldn't. I made this choice, but I was also the one he married. He should still love me! Before I could tighten my hold, the coin flipped over.

I staggered back, looking at Remy, then down at myself. I heard all of what Kazan said, all I said. This was insane. If what she said was true, I was never real. "Remy?"

I started to cry at the anger in his eyes, towards her, towards me. Not a trickle, no… gushing rivulets dripping down onto my hospital robe, turning it an even uglier shade of blue. "It's me!"

Remy caught me as the coin spun wildly. His hold on me only brought the tears on harder. Her, me, her, me. Kazan, Batista. Everything spun so fast it felt like we would split, not into two pieces, but a million. His arms clamped down around both of us.

CHAPTER FIVE

Tucked against his chest, I didn't want to think, though I had no choice. Who was I right now? In my head I looked for the coin, for what side it landed on, but it wasn't in the place I kept it. Was this part of the integration, I'd lose my image marker?

I must have stirred as Remy's hand slipped down my back, trying to comfort me. I trembled. This is what Schaeffer intended, using Remy to hold the fractions of me together as my brain reconciled itself. But would Remy stay?

I slid out of his arms. "Remy, I'm sorry. I'll figure out how to make this right."

Remy studied me. At least the anger was gone. "No, we'll figure it out. No more secrets."

"No more. I promise." He gave me a hug and let me get up.

I tried not to notice his frown as I dressed. This uniform wasn't what he was used to, nor the rank stitched onto my collar. The fact the uniforms were here waiting for me cemented the reality I'd led a double life.

I felt a twinge and winced, enough that he saw. He was at my shoulders, his hands gripping them as I rubbed my temple. "I thought you said you're not sick."

"I'm not." I let go of my face. "You're not the only one who has to get used to me. Right now I'm carrying around both my personalities. Until they merge back together, they're running into each other, and not too politely. They both want to be in charge." I turned to look him directly in the eyes, then stretched up to kiss him.

I half expected him to pull away, or at least ask which of us was present, but he kissed me back. After a few seconds the twinges dissolved.

Just about when it seemed this might go further, a beeping of the room's comm system interrupted us. Reluctantly I pulled my lips away from his. "Yes, this is… Kazan."

"Colonel, just a reminder the mission briefing will be…"

"Yes, I'll… we'll be there. Tell Col. Schaeffer that Maj. Battista will be attending, after we check on our other guest." There was no response. "Is there a problem, Ensign?"

"No, ma'am. I will relay the information." The line closed.

Remy was frowning again, not a look I liked to see. "Let's find Lizzy. Unfortunately we're gonna get Pissy Lizzy."

"Oh fun, like I don't have enough of your personalities to deal with." He smiled tensely. "I guess if I'm to be trapped with both of you, for God knows how long, I better get used to it."

Outside in the corridor a soldier stood at attention. "Take me to see Ms. Salazar." I got a nod and the soldier started aft.

Remy walked beside me, but his fingers brushed the walls. One eyebrow twitched. "What class of ship is this? I don't recognize the materials." As an engineer, he knew all the ships in the fleet, and this wasn't one of them.

"It's a… prototype." While the corridor was fairly standard, the metal wasn't, but I was used to its odd shimmer. "You'll get a full tour after we find Lizzy."

When the soldier stopped unexpectedly beside a cabin door, heat surged up inside me. I tapped at my comm. "Schaeffer, come in."

He answered almost immediately.

"Schaef, you son-of-a-bitch. I'm about to let this woman out and I'm gonna sic her on you. You better have a proper room ready before we get there."

I cut the link before he could respond and waved my hand over the access panel. The door slid silently open. If not for the change in lighting, Lizzy might not have noticed.

She sat cross-legged on a narrow bunk, reading. "About fucking time." She uncurled her legs and tossed a book onto the bunk as she stood. "How you feeling?" She gave me a hug.

"They got my headaches straightened out. I'm sorry you got sucked into this, and that they were so inhospitable. I'm fixing that right now."

"Whatever 'this' is. I don't care, as long as you're all right." Lizzy hugged me again, sighed in relief, then suddenly stiffened up. "Now, seriously. Has he been standing outside my room all this time?"

She let go, giving the soldier in the corridor an obvious up and down once-over. "Come here, Big Boy. I gotta thing for a man in uniform, especially getting him out of it."

The soldier turned a little pink in the cheeks and held his ground, until she took a couple swaying steps his direction, licking her lips wickedly. He took a step backwards, his eyes jerked in my direction. "Ma'am?"

I grabbed Lizzy by the back of her shirt, bra strap and all. “Rein it in girl.” I gave her a pull backwards. “I already promised to turn you loose on the guy who put you in here.”

“Ahhh, come on! I’ve been pinned up in here for days.” She pawed a hand at the soldier. “Twenty minutes.” Lizzy gave the soldier a lip-lick, achieving a red-hot glow over his whole face

I resisted laughing as I dragged her out of the cell, keeping myself between her and her victim. “Okay, ten minutes.” She blew him a kiss as I pulled her down the corridor. “Come find me later, Sweetie.”

I looked back at the traumatized soldier. “I’ll take her from here. Dismissed.”

“Yes, ma’am. Thank you, ma’am.”

Remy fell in behind us, snickering behind tight lips. When Lizzy got riled up, her wicked sense of humor kicked in. She became a little fireball, embarrassing innocent victims or slicing apart the egos of sleaze-balls. I was looking forward to what she’d do to Schaeffer.

At the approach of more soldiers, I jerked Lizzy back before she got a foothold. “Cool your jets. These boys have a job to do.”

“Oh… and Mr. Jail Warden doesn’t?” She fell back into stride.

I gave her a shrug. “Sometimes he needs to be reminded to treat guests better. I’m sure you can give him an etiquette lesson much more effectively than I can.”

“Oh, goody!” Her low laugh was genuinely evil, proving Lizzy still had her priorities in order. First, good sex. Second, tormenting men. Third, writing. Schaeffer had no idea how vicious Lizzy could be accomplishing her second task in life.

Not trying to pounce on the passing soldiers, she focused on me again. "So, what's with the weird new uniform, and this?" Lizzy flipped my collar tabs. "You're suddenly a colonel? Who are these guys and why am I here?"

She touched her own neck. "They shot me up with drugs. I didn't feel a thing until I woke up. It was like… out of one of those stupid spy movies."

"No so stupid." Remy edged in, the corridors wide enough for all three of us. "Seems our dear Shara isn't who she wanted us to think. She had a lot of secrets and they were unraveling downside."

"What? She really is a spy?" Lizzy grinned and crooned. "Do-do do-do, do-do do-do."

Remy snickered again and I looked up at him. A memory flashed back for me. "They didn't drug you. What did Schaeffer say to get you to come along?"

There was his scowl. "Let's just say mutual threats were exchanged. He notified Dr. Parsons you'd been contaminated by some toxin, ran bogus tests on her and her staff, then transferred the three of us out to a 'prepared facility' for treatment."

He did well not telling Lizzy he'd been afforded the comfort of my quarters, while she got the brig. I didn't say anything as Remy further explained my subterfuge all these years.

Lizzy took it a lot more easily than Remy, practically shrugging it off. "Makes sense. I noticed something different after you were married, but told myself that was the reason. I mean, no matter how long you live together, everything changes with the rings." She jabbed my ribs. "Tsk, tsk, tsk, secrets like this aren't allowed in marriage."

"They're not allowed between best-friend-sisters either." Remy scowled.

"Hah! Please!" Lizzy rolled her head back at Remy. "We have the biggest secrets, that aren't secrets, we just never talk about them."

She saw the confused look on his face. "I knew Shara would marry you before she did. With other boyfriends I knew which were good in…" She dodged my elbow. "…kissing."

She said it with a wink even Remy couldn't misinterpret. "She never talked about you, so you were her Prince Charming."

She dodged my hand, laughing as she bounced off the wall and slipped behind Remy for protection. "Figured you had to be a real toe-curler to make her change so much in just one year."

Remy blushed, but enjoyed her ribbing at my expense. "Chill it, Sis, or I'll put you back in isolation." The open corridors were too public for me.

"To hell with that! I didn't ask to come on this ride. Oh yummm, happy hour." Lizzy darted towards two approaching soldiers.

She slid to a stop between them, pulled her shoulders back and popped her breasts out. "My, my, my, all the pretty boys. You two want to come back to my place?" She shimmied for them, grinning.

I wanted to crawl under the decking. "Remy, please."

He laughed as he sprinted up and pulled Lizzy off the two men. He covered her mouth when she started to protest. Just then the doors beside us opened and over his hand I saw Lizzy's eyes widen.

CHAPTER SIX

Schaeffer stepped out into the corridor. “What the hell is going on out here?” His eyes fell on Remy, then down at Lizzy hanging from his arm.

“YEOW!” Remy dropped all five-foot-two of her and she landed like a cat, on her feet and prowling her next bird. Remy clutched his hand. “She bit me!”

If she had a tail, it would be flicking. I stepped up beside her. “Col. Richard Schaeffer, meet my friend, Lizzy Salazar.”

“Elizabeth, to you.”

Schaeffer started to give her a bow, but only managed to line himself up for the full-force flat of her hand against his cheek.

I had to give him points for not flinching. He simply stepped aside and allowed her entry into the conference room. “I apologize, Ms. Salazar, for your unsatisfactory accommodations. The situation has been corrected.”

He gave me a glare as I followed her in. I pointed her to a chair, Remy to another as I walked around the table set for two. The ensigns assigned to the briefing were already breaking out more place settings.

Schaeffer waited until they were finished before joining us, taking the seat opposite me. "I hadn't planned on…entertaining."

"Then, Dick, you should have left me to my reunion, or at least been nicer." Lizzy snipped at him.

Schaeffer shifted his glare to her. "Would you have preferred not knowing if you'd ever see your friend alive again?"

She met him glare for glare, hers still the stalking feline. "No, Dick, but you would have found me cooperative to almost anything, if you'd asked."

Did the fingerprints on his cheek just go a shade darker? I tried not to stare as they silently threw death-rays at each other. Fortunately the ensigns arrived with the first course. Schaeffer broke off the show-down. "Please proceed with serving. Our guests no doubt would appreciate a meal before returning to their quarters."

Food! I dug into my first meal in days. Apparently Lizzy felt the same way, quelling her need for vengeance for real food.

I felt much better and ready to talk business as the last dishes were cleared. I looked to Remy, then Lizzy. "I really do need to find out why I'm here. I promise, as soon as we're done here, I'll explain about all this, about me."

"Sure! We'll leave you and Dick to talk." Lizzy agreed, not taking any additional shots at Schaeffer. Deep down that had me worried. She was more dangerous when she was quiet.

Schaeffer watched Lizzy walk away from the table, or rather sashay. She always knew when a man was looking, especially one in her cross-hairs. He looked away as she glanced over her shoulder.

She caught him anyway and winked at me. Maybe her focused on tormenting him was a good thing. The crew would be relatively safe.

Relatively. “Remy, keep an eye on Lizzy? You’re free to take a look around before going back to our room.”

“Sure…” Remy said it with some hesitancy, but didn’t argue about leaving. Throughout the meal he’d been staring around the room, at the shimmering walls. He was more than happy to wander around the ship while I suffered a meeting.

At least he’d be in a good mood later. That thought got my toes curling. I watched him leave.

“Ah…hemm!” Schaeffer cleared his throat, bringing my imagination back to the present. “Now that we’ve dispensed with my punishment, can we get on with it?”

“Schaef, honey, don’t think the punishment’s over.” I folded my hands before me. “But let’s talk mission. You said the LR were behaving oddly? Pissed I left? Sounds sentient to me.”

“Okay, we’ve covered the possibility I might be wrong, but they’re still not rocket scientists. Though not dumb as rocks, or your dog.” He shook his head. “Zebra? Really? All this over a dog.”

“I was a kid. To me he was as big as a horse and had black stripes, like a zebra. They do too, hence the association. Can we move on?”

“Well, reports have it that once the LR realized you really were gone, they became agitated, even aggressive. They won’t have anything to do with the team and charge at them whenever they get too far from the camp.” He reached out to the hologram projector in the center of the table.

A view of LR-442 popped up, a totally virgin wilderness. The hologram didn’t do it justice. He tapped the audio and the room filled with a strange howling. He let it run for a few more seconds, before shutting it down.

"What is that?"

"Your team thinks they're mourning." Now it was Schaeffer's turn to be smug. "We were almost restocked when the reports came in. With this behavior the mission's at a stand-still. Since you're the only person they've responded to, you're going back, indefinitely."

A dozen responses popped in my head, but nothing came out of my mouth. My Kazan-side focused on the LR and I couldn't wait to get back. My Batista-side paralyzed me. Remy. I couldn't leave him again, not for that long, not anymore. We had plans. A family…

Wait! That life was a lie. Half our lives together was a lie. He thought I was off looking for DNA mutations. The other half of our lives, I was his wife. I loved him. I couldn't keep lying to him. I couldn't throw it away, not for anything.

I could feel them both in my head, starting to mesh, then breaking apart, like now. I rubbed my forehead as the coin spun. It landed, but I refused to see which side was up. I made a promise.

"No!" I pushed away from the table. "I split myself for ten years. It isn't fair to Remy, or me. We want a real life. I won't put it off 'indefinitely', not for anything. I'll resign first."

"Can't do that till we get back." Schaeffer put on that smug smirk. "We'll be there in a couple days. I can't imagine your guests would appreciate coming this far, only to be confined to the ship because you quit."

"I can imagine how pissed they'll be to see a new world, only to have you wipe out their memories of it."

Still the smirk. "So, what if there's no conditioning for them or you?" When I didn't answer it was his turn to push away from the table. "You've got three days to be rested and ready."

He left, but I remained.

I needed to think, without everyone asking questions and looking at me like I was an alien life form. I couldn't answer their demands if I barely knew who I was right now.

I recalled all the years I'd been out here alone, secretly. Our whole Corps, a secret. Almost fifteen years of secrets. I laid my head on the table, letting memories flood over me of all the missions and all the homecomings, Kazan and Batista.

My image marker, the coin, was tumbling wildly as I tried to shove my two lives into one. Which one was I going to be, or would I turn into someone completely different?

I got up from the table, nervous with that idea, all my memories getting jumbled together. They'd never be able to sort them out again. Was that why I wasn't a candidate anymore? Would they really leave my memories intact this time? Or Remy and Lizzy's? I couldn't be sure, but I had to pass the offer on, give them a choice.

First I had to find them.

CHAPTER SEVEN

The task of finding my friend and husband was simpler than I thought. I only had to follow the shell-shocked backward glances of soldiers I passed. Lizzy had that effect when running rampant. I passed a young captain, her cheeks still blushed.

"Our guests?" I queried to the forward day room.

"Yes, ma'am, and you'd better hurry." She went on, laughing.

I found Lizzy propped up on the bar. Not at the bar. On the bar, between two soldiers. She saw me and winked, letting her hand fall upon one of the soldier's buzz cut. She wriggled her fingers. "Ummm, velvety. I could be tempted to run more than my fingers over this." She scruffled the other soldier's head too, purring. "I'm thinking stereo."

"Ms. Salazar! If you would join me, I'll give you a tour." Her two somewhat willing victims turned to see me and jumped to attention.

"I'm doing fine on my own. If I get lost, I'm sure someone will be happy to escort me back to my room."

I gave her the look I'd learned from her mother.

She rolled her eyes. "Ooookay." She dropped her hands to the men's shoulders and launched herself off the bar. She bounced lightly. “I looovvve this lower gravity thing.” She continued little bouncy steps towards me, but not for my benefit. “I’ll see you later, boys.”

Remy joined me from where he’d been sitting in the corner. “I thought you were watching her.” I herded them both out of the day room.

“I was.” He grinned.

“And I was watching him too.” Lizzy chirped.

They both sounded like kids, backing each other up. “Fine. I’ll define ‘watch’ later. Right now I need to get you up to speed with what’s going on. We’ll start on the bridge.”

I led the way, speaking almost non-stop, even when we reached the bridge. They stared in total shock at the star field, reduced to a blur by FTL. We had real FTL, though 99.99 percent of Earth had no idea.

I started with the abridged version of history. “As you know, after NASA there was the PSTI. The Private Space Travel Industry led the next charge into space exploration. However, thanks to the 1967 U.N. Outer Space Treaty, ownership of the moon and planets in our solar system couldn’t go private.”

“Yeah. Space wasn’t going to be a repeat of the wild west days with land grabs and range wars running rampant.” Remy chimed in. “The Earth’s governments created the U.N. Space Alliance.”

“And with PSTI technologies, Peary Moon Base was founded. Resources mined from the moon funded new space stations and research into colonization of Mars, Venus, and various moons. However, it was always dreamed of going further.”

Remy finally took his eyes off the stars to look around the bridge. “And we have? How? Why don’t I… why doesn’t anyone know about this?” He turned back to me, looking me up and down, at the different uniform. "Are you still Alliance?"

"We are." I turned to look at the stars myself. "For hundreds of years we speculated about other solar systems, other planets. In the 21st century we started identifying possible worlds, getting better and better at finding near-Earths, but still couldn't get to them. In the last hundred years we developed the technology to attain FTL, but struggled finding materials capable of handling the stress. Imagine how surprised we were to find it right under our feet, at Peary."

I shifted back to Remy, feeling bad for him as an engineer, to be excluded from all this. I could see it in his eyes. Doubled by the fact that I knew, all this time.

The wife side of me stirred, but I needed to get this story told. "The discovery was before our time, but in one of the moon's asteroid craters they found a new iron ore compound. It had the lightness and strength they'd been looking for, but quantities were so limited the discovery was kept secret."

His resentment went down a notch.

"They'd found the missing element for building FTL ships. They still couldn't tell anyone. Instead, an ultra-secret division of the Corps was created for exploration outside our solar system. They were missioned with finding habitable planets, but more importantly, finding more of this elusive ore. Once they could get to other worlds, they put together research teams to study them. That's why I was recruited."

Remy's resentment notched up again. How many times had he mournfully postulated on the impossibility of ever achieving FTL, while the whole time I was planet hopping.

Lizzy sat in a chair, her hands tucked under her, for once afraid to touch anything. For her this was straight out of a

Sci-Fi movie. She spun her chair around. “So, Sis, how’d you get roped into this and what’s your job here?”

“Well, I did start out an astro-biologist, but I was recruited to become a Xeno-biologist. Now I’m a Xenologist.”

“A Xenologist?” Remy shook his head at me. “What’s the difference?”

“She holds a Master in all disciplines of studying alien life forms.” Schaeffer stepped onto the bridge.

Lizzy’s eyes lit up as she spun her chair around, her mind as sharp as her tongue. “Wouldn’t that require alien lives to master over, Dick?”

Schaeffer’s eyes flashed, a real flare of anger. “It’s Col. Richard Schaeffer.”

Lizzy gave a rolling shrug of her shoulder. “Same difference.” She coyly coiled a strand of hair between her fingers. “So, how’s that work, a master of aliens. Wouldn’t you need aliens?”

Schaeffer didn’t answer her, leaving the air quiet. Everyone on the bridge remained quiet, and here it came, that smirk when he was hiding something he wanted me to fish out. Only he was aiming it at Lizzy.

Remy realized what wasn’t being said. Amused surrealism turned to shocked betrayal as my secrets only got bigger with every breath. Lizzy spun around to glare at me too.

I couldn’t look at them. “We’ve been researching a planet that gave off the geo-chemical signatures of the ore we’re seeking. My unit is tasked with determining the sentience of its life forms and the effect of human colonization on its xeno-ecologies.”

Schaeffer strolled slowly around the upper ring. “In other words, imagine an alien race visiting Earth during our tree-swinging days. What if they determined we had no potential for sentience and settled down there?" Still smirking. "Or maybe they did and experimented to see what a little tweak here or there might produce out of our ape ancestors."

Geez… he loved that particular theory. Of course I couldn't debunk it. "Yes, my job is to make sure we don't upset the evolution of any indigenous intelligent creatures."

"So, Dick…" Lizzy spun her chair around again. "… am I going to get to see aliens? You better tell me yes, after kidnapping me."

"Depends on whether I throw you back in the brig." Schaeffer made the circuit, tossing the threat over his shoulder as he turned back to the door. "I suggest playing nice, Dizzi Lizzi."

"Sure thing, Captain Dick." She shouted after him, but got no response… from him.

The woman sitting quietly at the bridge's center console turned around. "Just so you know, Ms. Salazar. I am the only Captain here. This is my ship. Col. Schaeffer is mission commander. Col. Kazan is the commander of the Xenos." She added a 'don't make that mistake again' smile that would do Lizzy's mom proud. "Now it is time for my crew to get back to work." She tipped her head to me. "Ma'am."

"Thank you for indulging us, Captain." I guided Remy and Lizzy out. Remy was dying to stay, but I was tired, even though I'd slept for three days. I managed to answer a few more questions before Remy's arm slipped around me.

He shushed Lizzy's endless chatter. She wasn't clueless, exchanging a glance with Remy.

"It takes a lot out of me to integrate." It was the best explanation I had.

We reached Lizzy's new quarters, only a few doors down from mine… ours, I grabbed her arm. "Seriously,

Lizzy, as much fun as it is, Schaeffer can be a real ass if you get on his bad side. Don't get too carried away harassing him. That goes especially true for the crew."

There went her 'I know' eye roll. "I'll go easy on the boys, but Dick was daring me back there, and you know I can't walk away from a dare." I contemplated giving her the mom stare, but I was simply too wiped out to pull it off.

She snickered as Remy led me to bed.

CHAPTER EIGHT

For almost a whole cycle I barely woke long enough to eat. Half-asleep, I heard Remy and Lizzy whispering, her giggling, probably telling him more escapades. When I finally regained consciousness, I let my Kazan side launch into briefings from my team.

I'd been gone less than a month, but they'd been in total shutdown. I'd hoped that in my absence the LR would redirect to another Xenologist, but leaving had the opposite effect.

I studied all the reports, trying to figure out what went wrong. Procedures were followed. We didn't trespass into the forest, but the LR were agitated and even claimed our meeting place, a rock about fifty yards from the forest edge.

I'd originally picked the rock for a place to sit. Day after day, month after month, nothing happened, except I got better at drawing landscapes. Then shortly after arriving on my last stint, I saw movement in the heavy brush between me and the forest edge. I felt their eyes and let them watch me draw. When I finished, I propped the picture on the rock and left.

The next morning I found a leaf full of berries in its place. I started a new picture and before I finished a rough outline, two LR appeared on the edge of my grass clearing, directly in the line of sight I'd selected. It was that day I knew they were sentient. They'd completed a trade and possessed enough self-awareness to want their picture drawn.

Each drawing, no matter how bad, drew them closer, and I talked. Not knowing what to say, I told Lizzy stories. I knew them well enough and drew pictures, naming everything in them, and my audience silently paid attention. I tried to encourage pictures from them, bringing out supplies of paper and charcoal. They took the supplies, but I never received a picture back, just lots more berries.

On the day I left, they gave no indication they understood I was leaving, even though I drew it out for them. But when I didn't show up, neither did the LR. For the first week they circled the edges of the forest, ignoring the Xeno who took my place. Then they aggressively drove him off the rock, repeatedly.

Not understanding this shift to aggression, our people were ordered to keep to the camp and lakeside. The LR keening from the forest haunted the little valley. Thermals showed LR sitting, watching the encampment. Waiting.

Now, as we approached LR-442, we'd find out if they were really waiting for me. I brought Remy and Lizzy to the bridge and they stood on either side of me, wide-eyed, jaws agape as we fell into orbit over the planet.

"There she is. LR-442." I held my hand out to the image filling our screens.

"Or Hippotigris, as some of us call her."

"LR-442!" I gave Schaeffer a glare.

He ignored me. "She's very near Earth standards. The differences are minute, except showing high levels of the resources we're looking for. So far we haven't detected any elements dangerous to human DNA."

"Except it's already inhabited." Remy leaned on the railing, his eyes fixed on the planet.

"And we get to live here for a while, get to meet the aliens?" Lizzy chirped at me, giving Schaeffer a sweet innocent smile that was anything but innocent. "When do we land this baby?"

"We don't. The shuttle leaves in two hours. You have the allowed property list. Be packed and ready. No exceptions or delays." Schaeffer turned to go, but stopped as he brushed against Lizzy's shoulder. "It would be a shame to miss your company because you were too busy catting around with the crew."

"Not a problem Cap…" She stopped herself. "…Commander Dick. You going to strip-search me for contraband, before I go down... with you?" She knew how to deliver her words, all sultry teasing.

I wanted to clamp my hand over her mouth, but it was too late. Remy did a throat-clearing to hide a laugh or groan.

A tick appeared in Schaeffer's eyelid. "Two hours!" His voice came out lower and huskier.

He stomped out and the captain turned her chair around. "Ms. Salazar! If your antics get you sent back up here, I'll confine you to quarters. Is that understood, Ms. Salazar, Col. Kazan?"

The captain's 'mom look' made Lizzy drop her head, though she still grinned. "Yes, ma'am. My apologies."

"And mine, Captain." I grabbed Lizzy by the back of her collar, dragging her with me. I continued the 'what have you been up to' stare we always got from her mom just before the shit hit the fan. "Is there anything I need to know?"

"Nope!"

Remy gave her the look too. He didn't believe her any more than I did.

"I promise. You can back off the Kazan." She wriggled out of my grip. "I'll watch my tongue when we get to the ground."

"Yeah, I'm sure half the crew would volunteer to watch it too." Remy couldn't help himself. "Can you at least try to keep it inside your own lips for a few hours?"

Lizzy opened her mouth again, mimicking what she could still do with his suggestion. I covered my eyes. "LIZZY, ENOUGH!"

All I got was her deep snickering. She loved it when I finally reached my Kazan limit, probably trying to urge Batista back. How I, or my other self, put up with this for so long baffled me, but we were as close as any two sisters could ever be. Surviving all our childhood escapades.

Now we were on a new escapade together. Dizzi Lizzi, Darin' Sharan and … Remy. I cringed to think what she named him. I gave her a shove inside her cabin, with strict orders to be on time, better yet, fifteen minutes early.

In our room, I did another full sweep and rechecked my list. Normally I was too well organized to give it a second thought. Normally I only packed for me. Normally I didn't have another personality in my head. "Well, we're ready with an hour to kill."

"Really?" Remy came up behind me, his arms pinned mine down. "In that case, I know exactly how to use it up."

"Remy, come on…" I struggled against his intentions, until his lips went straight to a weak point in the curve of my neck. There went the coin, along with my knees. There went his hands, and there went what was left of my will as the Batista he knew surfaced.

He had his own evil snicker, when he knew he got his way, even more evil when he knew he'd drawn out the wife side of me. In this lighter gravity, he easily carried me to the bunk barely wide enough for two, and made good use of the tight space and our spare time.

He left me scurrying to regain my Kazan side and get dressed again. LR didn't like uniforms, so I opted for jeans and a little white undershirt. Only my ball cap had name and rank on it. I pulled it on as the door buzzed. Remy already had our duffle bags over his shoulders.

Lizzy stood outside. "What took you so long?"

I tried to ignore the heat in my cheeks as I glanced at my watch. Fifteen minutes. "Ready to meet your first aliens? Where's your bag? Need help with it?"

"Nooo…" She waved me off. "A sweet young thing came and got it." She grinned at Remy standing behind me. "Hope you got enough of her. Last time I went camping, it wasn't very private. Everybody hears everything."

I pushed her out the door. "We're not sleeping in lean-tos." I pointed her aft. "Before we leave, I need to know you understand the rules."

Lizzy looked up at me with her 'I'm smarter than you give me credit for' glance. "I know this is important. Once we hit dirt, Loosey Lizzy will be temporarily retired."

An unexpected wave of relief rushed over me, Batista telling me she meant every word. When had I stopped trusting her to do the right thing? Was it just living split in two for so long? I wrapped my arm around her shoulders. "I'm sure this adventure will be worth the sacrifice."

We reached the shuttle with almost ten minutes to spare. Lizzy popped up behind members of the team waiting on the ramp. A few of the men flinched. Several of the women grinned, including the one checking off our duffel bags.

Remy noticed. "What is it you women think is so funny? I'd think you'd be throwing a fit with her inappropriate conduct."

“Major. Do you realize how many years, centuries, we’ve put up with the reverse?” She resisted a total eye roll. “To us, she’s cute, funny and makes them feel totally… adolescent. To them, she’s the fox and they’re the chickens. Best of all, she’s a civilian and under the circumstances no one can charge her with sexual harassment.”

“Well, I hope you don’t have a guy in the crew, unless you’re comfortable letting her screw with… his head.” Remy tossed our scanned and tagged bags in the cargo container.

“He wishes. Lizzy stays away from the ones spoken for.” Being the last of the away party, she closed the container and gave the handler permission to load. “All aboard!” She shooed us up the ramp.

We made our way to the front of the shuttle. Lizzy had already seized a seat directly across from Schaeffer. We took the other two lead seats. I looked back at the contingent. “It’s too soon for rotations. Why we upping our presence?”

Schaeffer spun his chair towards me. “Your leaving caused a change in their behavior. Hopefully your return will bring a calming response. We need to be prepared, either way. You just worry about getting the LR cooperating again.”

“What about me, Dick?” Lizzy chirped. “What do you expect me to do?”

Schaeffer shifted his eyes her direction. “Behave and keep the colonel happy.”

Tick, tick, tick. I inhaled as the machine in Lizzy’s head went into free-spin. Remy rubbed between his eyes as her mouth opened. “Shara don’t swing that way, unless you’re talking about yourself. In that case you can blow…”

“Lizzy!”

“What?” Her fists clenched in frustration. “We’re not on the ground yet.”

“Shut up or I’ll lock you up myself.” I tipped my head back to the crew, hoping Schaeffer had engaged white noise. Lizzy spun her chair around to face the window.

Schaeffer frowned. Maybe he was reconsidering bringing Lizzy along. He looked over at Remy. “If you’ll excuse us...” It wasn’t a request.

Schaeffer tapped controls on his armrest and closed the curtain of white noise to surround just the two of us. “I appreciate you taming her, but not at your expense. She’s family and until you’re fully integrated, I need you focused.” He glanced at Lizzy pouting. “She’s here, use her. If she’s busy she’ll stay out of trouble.”

“I don’t know, Schaef. She’s still got a serious score to settle. I’d watch your back, among other body parts.”

His eye twitched again. “You let me worry about my body parts.”

Somehow that was reassuring to both sides of my head. Despite how I razzed Schaeffer, he was a partner I trusted and could predict. If he wasn’t worried about her, I shouldn’t be either. I did my best to relax for the ride down.

CHAPTER NINE

In my head Kazan played out the plan. We'd settle into camp, then I'd approach the meeting rock alone. If accepted back, I'd start working at bringing in other people.

Schaeffer agreed. He'd studied enough psychology to understand pack theory. Social beings were pack animals. A pack approach, with my real pack, might be what we needed.

I theorized in my head, until the lights on our arm consoles lit up. We were about to land. I turned to look out the window I shared with Remy.

As I looked down at the canopy of treetops, I remembered an art class in high school, and being criticized over my choices in greens and blues. The teacher was adamant my hues never existed in nature. She'd eat her words if she saw this. The vibrancy below was dazzling.

I looked over at Lizzy. Her nose was pressed against the portal in excitement. Schaeffer reached over and patted her knee, getting a quick but genuine smile from her, before another 'ahhh' sight opened up before her. Maybe there was hope after all.

I went back to my own amazements. Feathery green trees wisped in the air turbulence we created. Foliage covered the foothills of towering mountains, thinning out at higher elevations to reveal purple-hued rock formations, resource abundant mountains. There.

I pointed it out to Remy, a waterfall calculated to be at least 3000 ft. He ‘ahhh’d as the forest suddenly revealed grassy meadows and a massive lake.

Remy and Lizzy never took their eyes off the views as the shuttle circled over the lakeshore. We landed smoothly on a wide rock shelf about 100 yards from camp.

I stood up, full Kazan now. “Okay team. For you newbies, it’s the equivalent of a Northern California summer out there, which means comfortable in the daytime, cold at night, possible fogbanks in the mornings. Stay near camp and out of the forests. If you see any of our native friends, sit down. By sitting you display passive posturing. Recent info is they’re agitated. If they appear so, calmly walk back towards the camp. Do not stare at them or be confrontational. This is their home, not ours. Understood?”

“Yes, ma’am!” The response was energetic. They were all excited to be back. With my nod, the back doors opened and the team filed out, lining up to wait for their gear and tent assignments.

In our group Schaeffer hit the ground first, Lizzy on his heels. He swung his arm to the view. “Welcome to Hippotigris.”

“Stop calling it that!” I stomped past him, Remy following. I heard Schaeffer snicker as he fell in too, Lizzy in tow.

As we reached the first row of tents, the camp manager trotted up to us. “Col. Kazan, Col. Schaeffer, welcome back. I have your quarters ready, as well as a tent for Ms. Salazar.”

He handed us each water bottles, giving Remy and Lizzy the speech. “Nothing is thrown away here. You refill these at the mess tent. There's a sterilization unit there to clean them. If you need anything, stop anyone and ask. We're fairly informal here. Think adult summer camp. If you see something you'd like to volunteer to work with, extra hands will be appreciated."

Remy took the bottle, his eyebrow peaking. "Pretty liberal attitude for a secret base."

The camp manager only smiled. "Not like you're going to sneak off and tell anyone." He turned back to me. "Ma'am, as soon as you're available, we're already getting increased thermals out there. It's like they know you've arrived."

"Well then, we'll drop gear and I'll head out to the rock."

The manager nodded, preceding us, pointing to larger structures in the center of tent city. "Mess, showers, laundry, supply, rec. center, outside of which is a large fire-pit. Yes, we have marshmallows and hotdogs, even graham crackers and Hershey's."

As we reached the housing sector, a soft sound echoed from the forest. Lizzy came to stand beside me. "What is that noise?"

I'd heard it about mid-camp. "It's them." I stared out towards the forest line. My Batista side was a bit scared, but Kazan held the coin right now. "I've never heard them like this. Can we get this over with? I have work to do."

The camp manager nodded, heading down a row of tents. "Ms. Salazar. Your quarters." He pulled open a door, motioning her inside.

She stopped at the door, tapping the side of the tent. It was a semi-rigid plastic, not the old style canvas. "Definitely not a lean-to." She peaked inside. "There's two cots. Am I sharing with someone?"

"No, it was requested you be housed alone." From the way he clamped his lips together, he was trying not to repeat what he'd really been told.

Lizzy's mouth opened, but she looked at me and contained her snide comment. "Well, I appreciate the courtesy. Thank you. Where's Shara's tent?"

The man nodded down the dirt avenue. "At the end of the row. Name's on the door. Col. Schaeffer is two lanes over." He held his hand to gesture her inside. "An ensign will be here any moment to help you settle in."

Lizzy looked to me and off to the forest. The keening only seemed to get louder. "You going out there now?"

I nodded. "Don't worry. I'll catch up as soon as I can. Get acquainted with the camp and behave yourself." I got her eye roll and she disappeared into the tent.

By the time we reached my tent, so had our duffels. The ensign carried them in and disappeared as I showed Remy the meager amenities of our new home.

He was not impressed, opening the lockers and trunks. "This is how you lived on all those TDYs?" He kicked at the cots. "No wonder it took a week to get you out of bed when you came home."

"Yeah, but you didn't complain." I went to the table, picking up one of my sketch pads and a charcoal pencil. "Unpack. If you need anything before I get back, go find the camp manager." I turned back around. "I need to let them know I'm back and see how they react."

Remy's eyebrows did their furrowing trick when he knew he was facing Kazan and not Batista. It didn't stop him from being concerned. "If they're agitated, is it safe to go out there?"

"I'm sure it is. I've got something of a relationship with them." I let Batista out enough to cross the few feet between us, stretching up to kiss him. "I'll be back."

CHAPTER TEN

My first time across this field, the wild grasses came up higher than my waist. Now a narrow path cut down to the soil. I was glad to see no one had ventured too far off it, leaving the meadow pristine.

I reached my rock. The area around it cleared by frequent visits, though I could see the last few weeks of disuse had allowed some of the grasses to recover. I climbed onto the rock and stood still, listening.

I'd only heard little sounds from them, of pleasure, excitement, and curiosity. Never the keening. Never this sound. I listened, trying to decipher it.

"Ara. They're calling you Ara."

I nearly fell off the rock, turning around to see Lizzy behind me. "You were supposed to stay in the camp. You need to go back or they might not come out."

Lizzy ducked down a little, nodding ahead of us. "I couldn't resist and it's too late now."

The grasses were moving, swaying, though I still couldn't see the LR. They didn't travel in straight lines, but wove their way towards their center of focus. I saw at least ten different disturbances. "Get behind me then. They might be aggressive."

Just as I issued a warning, several heads popped over the grass, the tops of the heads only. Between pointy ears cocked in our direction were thick v-shaped black tufts of fur that stood straight up. The bottom of the V was still hidden by the grasses, but not the eyes. Huge golden, intense eyes stared at me.

Seeing Lizzy with me, I thought they'd dart back towards the woods, but they kept coming. I held my breath as the grass stopped waving and slowly one head eased into the clearing. A muscular body stealthfully followed on powerful thick legs.

The tuft that crowned its head continued down the spine to the hindquarters. Black stripes flowed down over the torso, into fur as golden as its eyes. The tufting reappeared down the back of each leg. The bottom of the v-tufted head ended in a broad nose, over a large mouth showing sharp protruding teeth. We still didn't know whether to call it a feline, canine or primate.

I leaned towards primate because of its eyes. Large and golden, they reminded me of a giant tarsier. Especially as it sat back and folded its front legs across a broad chest, displaying long fingers instead of paws. It let out a cooing sound and another creature exited the grass from the same path, this one slightly smaller with no tufts.

I recognized both of them, the pair that visited me almost daily. She wasn't as cautious as her mate, coming up to me boldly. She stood and nuzzled my cheek, much more vigorously than usual, nearly toppling me off the rock.

Several more pairs entered the circle, the females giving me the same greeting. Their strange song rose higher and louder.

The first female stayed in front of me, her head tipped from side to side, her eyes almost seemed to be asking me something. "Arrrraaaa. Arrrraaaa." The male came to stand beside her, giving me the same forlorn look.

Shara. Ara. Maybe Lizzy was right. Their first word, after so many attempts to communicate, made me somewhat embarrassed. I pressed my hand to my chest. "Shara." I reached out slowly towards the male's chest.

He backed away and the female's long digits wrapped around my hand, touching it to her chest. "Yinet." She pushed my hand back to my chest. "Ara." Her chest. "Yinet."

"Told ya. Ara, Shara, oops!" Lizzy grabbed my leg as the female shot her head around me. Her neck extended, sniffing at Lizzy, pulling back quickly, then sniffing again.

In a movement I still found disturbing, her head rotated around completely, like the Tarsier. The other females surrounded Lizzy, sniffing at her. Lizzy's eyes started to look like theirs, huge and bulging. The female swung her head back, nearly nose to nose with Lizzy. "Yinet."

"Ahhhh…Shara, what does she want?"

"Your name, silly. Do what I did." I had to practically pry Lizzy's fingers out of my thigh. I turned around to face Yinet. Maybe the pack theory was right.

"Oookay." Lizzy pointed to herself. "Lizzy. I'm Lizzy."

"Litty. Litty." Yinet jabbed at Lizzy's chest, then popped back up to me. "Litty." The other LR picked it up, bouncing around the circle.

"Shara, why are they so excited? I'm not real thrilled about being on tonight's menu." Lizzy's fingers dug into my leg again.

"Stay calm, I think they recognize your name from the picture stories I told them." Now that I'd been greeted, I sat down on the rock, Lizzy crowding up next to me. The male sat down too, so I pointed to myself again. "Shara." I pointed at him, but he cocked his head at me, chirping in a quizzical tone.

I started to point at him again, but Yinet stepped between us, spouting out a string of chirps and guttural noises. She leaned her head out, doing that sniffing thing again, up and down my body.

This time it seemed so specific, I considered taking a whiff too. Did I smell offensive? Suddenly she stood up on her hind legs. Her nose twitched vigorously as she looked back towards the camp.

Her head spun around towards her mate and she chattered at him. He approached and started the same snorting. While not as intrusive, I was getting offended. Suddenly he darted back into the grasses.

I stood up on the rock again and saw the sway of the stalks. He wasn't heading towards the forest. No, he was heading towards camp. No, towards a small group of observers. Lizzy wasn't the only one who'd tried to follow me. There was the colonel and Remy.

Oh, crap. "Schaef, we got one coming your way. Remain calm. Don't react, unless he gets aggressive. Then just retreat."

I tried to keep my voice low. They'd never done this before. To my surprise, Yinet climbed up on the rock with me, staring back at my camp. From the way my people started to turn in circles, I knew her mate was already there. They were fast on all fours.

"Shara?" Lizzy gripped at my leg again as several LR again started their sniffing and nuzzling, purring her name.

"You're fine, just keep telling them your name, and pay attention to theirs."

"How, they're all the same. Lizzy. Lizzy. Oh, we need to introduce them to breath mints. Hey, where's that one going?"

I looked down in time to see tufted heels disappear into the grass. “Another male heading your way.” I bit at my lip, wondering what all this meant. I stretched to look back at the camp. I squinted.

Yinet’s mate suddenly loomed tall over the men, then his head darted out.

“Owww!” I heard Remy over my comm. “Shara, I’m trying hard not to react, but I don’t appreciate the head butting over here. What the hell is going on, and why’s he growling at me?”

“Are you sure he’s growling? What’s it sound like?”

“It sounds like growling, like… grrrr…ret… Oh? Gerret? Ah, he stopped hitting me.”

“Well, it might be his name. Introduce yourself and see if he repeats you.”

“Okay. Gerret… Rem…my. Yeah, Remy. Remy… Oh Shit!” As I watched, Remy disappeared. I could see a flailing arm or leg as he was dragged off his feet and into the grass. My hand clenched, Batista trying to get out. I couldn’t let her, she’d panic.

Just then another LR stood over the group, his nose roving about before he started butting his head against Schaeffer. “Kazan?” For the first time Schaeffer sounded genuinely alarmed.

I could see Remy on his feet again, walking or being pulled towards us. “Introduce yourself and start this direction. Use your first name. They can’t pronounce ‘s’ sounds.”

“Dick should be easy for them.”

“Shut up, Lizzy.” Schaeffer stuck with Richard, avoiding the tumble by heading towards us willingly.

The LR next to Lizzy heard her name over the little speaker on her belt and got excited, chattering at it. Great, there went our open comm line.

Remy entered the clearing, Gerret's marsupial fingers wrapped firmly around his arm. He was dragged right up to my rock, where both he and Yinet resumed snuffing at us and chittering to one another. I suddenly wanted to crawl under the rock in embarrassment.

"Want to tell me what's going on?" Remy's tone said he really was trying not to be rude.

"Not yet." I looked at Gerret and spoke his name. Now he chattered excitedly, bouncing off the rock with Yinet. They made a circle of the clearing before sitting down together.

Schaeffer stumbled into the circle and was thrust towards Lizzy. That male bounced around the circle. "Rikerd. Rikerd. Rikerd."

"Richard, what did he introduce himself as?"

Schaeffer, all stiff and composed, shifted his eyes to me. "Belup. We seemed to agree on that pronunciation."

"She's Kenup. Seems there's a naming thing for mates." Lizzy looked at the male. "Nice to meet you, Belup." That elicited an excited reaction.

I glared down at Lizzy from my place on the rock. "Now, is there anything you want to tell me?" Getting nothing, I had to fight not being totally pissed off. "All the sniffing around was to see who… marked who."

Lizzy's cheeks turned red. Schaeffer's lips got tighter.

Remy caught on, looking over Lizzy's head to the camp. "I suppose it could be worse if they got a whiff of the crew."

"I never… not this time." Lizzy turned nearly purple.

"So, Dick, how long did it take her to get under your sheets?"

"Not long. She was easy. Ouch!"

Lizzy nailed his shin perfectly.

The LR started to keen at the tension. I took a deep breath and let it out slowly. "We'll discuss this later. You better sit down." I pulled Remy down on the rock beside me. Schaeffer and Lizzy sat on the ground and immediately the LR calmed down.

As disturbing as it was, it revealed LR formalities. Females could speak to females, males with males, and mated pairs with each other, otherwise the sexes sat in clusters of bachelors and bachelorettes.

Our xeno-sociologists would have fun figuring this out, later. For now I needed to continue communications.

I started by pointing at things around us. It amused the LR and we played the naming game for a good hour, until they grew fidgety.

I knew it was time for us to part when Yinet came to me again and nuzzled my cheek. "Yes, Yinet." I pointed at the sun and circled my finger across the sky and back to its morning position. "Tomorrow."

I pointed to the rock beneath me. "Tomorrow."

"Tomrow." She took my hand and pointed to the forest. "Ara, Yinet." Her long fingers pointed to the others in my group, then to the forest. "Tomrow."

All I could do was nod my head. Was she really inviting me into their forbidden territory? She let me go and ran off into the deep grasses. I was in.

CHAPTER ELEVEN

We were accepted, though it opened up a larger mess for me to deal with. I turned my attention back to Lizzy and Schaeffer. "Seriously?"

Our distraction with the LR gave Lizzy time to recover. "Last time I checked it wasn't illegal to screw your kidnapper, though the opposite's a felony. Besides, you threw me at him."

"You did!" Remy and Schaeffer spoke in unison.

"What happens in a week when you get bored?" Being Kazan, I knew everything in Lizzy's history. "I have to work with this guy. He's a big enough pain in the ass without you screwing with his head."

"We're adults, so that's our business. Who knows, maybe he won't be such a pain in your ass, if he's my pain in the ass for a while."

Her cheeks flamed as her words replayed in her head. "Shut up, Remy. You too, Dick!" She stood up and stomped back towards camp.

Schaeffer squashed his comeback. "Listen Kazan, it happened. Drop it." At least he didn't stomp off pissed, not that I felt any better.

I felt worse, Batista digging at my conscience. Crisis over, my sides started to turn again. I told Lizzy to have fun with him. I never thought she'd actually get involved.

Remy watched them leave too. "Don't worry. Actually, this might be a good thing."

"I don't know." Schaeffer caught up with Lizzy and wrapped his arm around her. "She's the 'catch and release' type."

"Yeah, well there's always a first." Remy pulled me from the rock and kissed me, then backed away. "Okay, I'm with Lizzy on the breath mints. Can we go wash off this LR funk?"

"I'll tell you what, there's a little cove up the lakeside. You game for skinny-dipping on an alien planet?"

Remy laughed, kissing me one more time.

⌘ ⌘ ⌘

I replayed the LR strange introductions to the Xeno team. Introducing Remy and Lizzy, as embarrassing as the episode was, revealed their social secrets and sentience. I left out how I reacted to Schaef and Lizzy.

I felt bad about it, but when Lizzy joined us for breakfast, she seemed to have forgotten the way we'd parted the day before.

She sat down bubbly as ever, not even complaining about reconstituted eggs. She just folded them into a slice of bread, a habit she had as a kid. She squirted her sandwich with ketchup as Schaeffer set his tray down.

He wrinkled his nose and she only smirked, nibbling on her egg sandwich. "So, I've been thinking. Since they seem to like art, can I do sketches while you do your thing?"

She reached into her backpack and pulled out a sketchpad. "I did these from the videos you were running."

I opened the book and she reached over to point at a male. I recognized immediately it was Gerret. "They're markings are distinct. See how his flow almost perfectly along his rib, while Belup's zags more horizontally. Yinet has a swirl right down the side of her neck. Kenup's stripes don't start until her shoulders."

She smiled knowingly. "I didn't get how they reminded you of Zebra, but I do now."

I didn't feel a twinge, maybe because I didn't have to explain it to her. I flipped through several pages of drawing, some with names attached, arrows pointing to the markings making each LR unique. "You did these last night? How?"

"Sweetie, I write children's books, duh! I'm also masochistic…" She reached over and plucked a grape from Schaeffer's tray, leering at him enough I could swear he blushed. "…about detail."

She realized it wasn't a grape as it oozed red liquid. She frowned, touched her tongue to the juice, then nibbled at the berry.

"It's local harvest. The LR let us pick them." Schaeffer split his bunch with her. "I guess we know what role Lizzy will fill. She was up half the night doodling."

"Don't complain. So were you."

Remy coughed up some of his artificial eggs, covering his mouth as Lizzy winked at me.

"Shhhh…" Schaeffer darted his eyes around to the other tables around us.

Lizzy grinned through a mouthful of berries, rubbed her shoulder affectionately against his, but looking at me. "We cool?"

"We're cool." Or getting there. "The pictures were good." She had an eye for the little details. "Draw to your heart's content. Maybe you can translate my ideas into pictures, and do the same for them."

I pushed my tray away. "We need to get a move on, if that was a real invitation yesterday." I took Remy's hand, and reached over to take Lizzy's. "Ready for a new adventure?"

Lizzy took Schaeffer's hand. "It's about time Lizzi and Sharan grew up."

Schaeffer seemed a bit awkward with the gesture, not the four musketeers' type, but he shrugged. "I guess I'm game."

"Ahh, there's a problem." Schaeffer raised a brow at me. "Both of us heading off into the deep, dark woods...?" Nada from him. "Protocol. Who'll be in charge back here?"

"All taken care of." Down went the brow. "Besides, if your theory on social order is correct, we have to go in pairs. Do you want to risk offending them?"

He had a point, but still, this was weird for me. Remy saved the awkward moment. "Well, since we don't know what they intend, we should be prepared for an overnighter. To that effect, I already asked the camp manager to prepare four camp packs. We just need to pick them up and add our personals."

I couldn't help but be surprised. He must have gone out after I fell asleep. "Okay, channeling your old boy scout?" He shrugged. "All right then, expedition leader is your job. Lizzy is our journalist. I guess that makes you security, Schaef."

He looked at Lizzy and smirked. "Yeah, someone has to keep Litty in check."

It all seemed to fit. In less than an hour we hiked out to the rock. We didn't even have to sit down before the LR slipped into the clearing. Yinet and Gerret were at the lead, giving us the nuzzle greeting, before guiding us towards the forest.

Unlike their usual routine, they didn't take the long-weaving route, instead headed straight into the trees. Once under a full canopy, all but Yinet and Gerret disappeared.

It took quite a while for me to realize where they went, but when I did, I couldn't help but stop to watch. The whole party stopped and Lizzy came to my side. "Ahhhh, Sis, you're seeing what I am?"

"Bear-sized flying Tarsiers?" It was incredible, something that size leaping effortlessly from tree to tree.

"Fascinating! I'd love to get a scan on them. Even if they have lightweight bones, sheer muscle mass should make that impossible. Oh…oh…ohhh!" Remy cringed as a large male missed one branch, did a somersault and caught another, to swing onto a heavier limb.

Schaeffer was speechless.

"We've got a lot of preconceived ideas to undo." I saw Yinet looking up too, pacing nervously as she waited for us. The ground wasn't their natural habitat, probably accounting for their odd approaches through the meadow. I waved my arm at my team. "Come on."

She cooed and held her arm out to us, her fingers fluttered. "Cumin, cumin." I couldn't help but appreciate how quickly she grasped words and gestures.

Everyone fell back in line, trying to keep our eyes on the ground beneath us, rather than on the highway over our heads. We needed to be careful with no paths to follow and only dim light breaking through the trees.

After several hours Yinet stopped by a stream. Gerret reappeared with LR bearing leaves filled with berries. It was a break we needed, especially Lizzy. Hiking wasn't her sport and the new government-issue boots were blistering her feet.

Even so, she didn't complain when Yinet urged us to continue. I caught Schaeffer's eye. He noticed Lizzy's limp too. Bringing up the rear, he'd help her out. All I could do was hope our route didn't get any rougher.

Of course it did. The deeper into the forest we went, the higher into the mountains. I kept checking on Lizzy and could see by late afternoon she wasn't able to take much more. Schaeffer helped her up the rocky path and offered to take her pack, but she was stubborn.

When Lizzy's eyes watered up, I turned to get Yinet's attention, but she and Gerret were gone over the rock wall above us. I looked up into the trees and there were no more flying LR. Remy moved past me, pulled himself up over the rock shelf. "Remy, where are the LR? Can you see them?"

"Yeah… I can see them." He stared at something for another few seconds before turning back to me. "You're not going to believe this." He started to reach for my hand, but looked past me. I followed his gaze and saw Lizzy barely clinging to the rocks below me, her face pale. Schaeffer steadied her. "Geez, pass Lizzy up to me, now."

She was ready to collapse. I hoisted my pack up to Remy and braced my feet in the boulders. I grabbed the straps at the top of her pack, giving Lizzy a pull up the wall while Schaeffer pushed. We got her high enough for Remy to lift her over the ledge. Schaeffer scrambled up after her and gave me a pull up. I joined him where Lizzy sat exhausted.

Remy already had her pack off and Schaeffer pressed a bottle of water at her. Her hands shook as she tried to drink and I could see her fingers were scraped from the rocks. Schaeffer took the bottle, holding it to her lips. I dug out a first aid kit. "I'll let Yinet know we have to make camp."

"I don't think that'll be an issue." Remy pointed up the mountain.

I turned to look at what mesmerized him and was drawn to my feet, drawn past Remy. “You two help Lizzy.”

“I can walk.” Lizzy protested, even as Schaeffer lifted her in his arms.

They followed me to where the trees opened up, revealing purpled-hued cliffs, terraced cliffs, carved cliffs. Cliff dwellings.

Not caves, but artfully carved, terraced homes. Immediately my mind went to ancient Petra in Jordan and to the intricately carved temples in Thailand. Did the LR do this? How? This place completely conflicted with the simplicity of life they’d let me see.

Sitting at the edges of the terraces were LR, hundreds of them. At the base of the cliffs, Yinet and Gerret sat upon a raised stone. Yinet’s long fingers wriggled and curled towards herself. “Ara. Cum.”

CHAPTER TWELVE

It wasn't often Lizzy was quiet, but then we all stood tongue-tied. Yinet beckoned and I had to break the trance to go to her.

Remy caught up with me, juggling our packs to grab my elbow, slowing me down. "Shara, do you think this is wise?"

"I've worked too hard winning their trust to lose it rejecting their hospitality." I pulled his hand free, but wove my fingers between his when my inner Batista protested. "Come on."

Remy hung onto my hand. Schaef fell in behind carrying Lizzy, despite her squirming around to look at the cliffs, at the LR, at Yinet. No doubt her artist mind absorbing every minute detail, despite her condition.

When we reached the stone dais, Yinet's fingers still fluttered at me. I interpreted it as an offer and reached out my hand as well. Remy resisted, but let go as her long digits, strong enough to break mine with the slightest squeeze, pulled me up onto the stone.

She made me sit on the stone bench beside her. I felt like a rag-doll next to her, but she invited the rest of my party up to join us. No sooner than we were seated, other LR appeared with more berries and water.

We ate ravenously, except Lizzy. She leaned against Schaeffer, trying to nibble on the berries, but too exhausted and hurting.

Seeing the raw sores on her hands and feet, a female LR approached with what looked like large leaves, but soaked until they were soft and mushy. She was polite, gesturing to Lizzy's feet and the leaves.

"Oh, okay." Lizzy flinched as the LR draped the first leaf around her foot. Tears welled up in her eyes. "Ahhh, that's good." She smiled and nodded, letting this impromptu doctor wrap both her feet.

Curious, Schaef pulled on the corner of a leaf, smashing it between his fingers, then rubbing it over the back of his hand. "Cooling, and some sort of analgesic quality. Hope there's no side-effects for humans."

"Nice that you bring that up now, but frankly, I don't care." Not suffering, she picked up a leaf of berries, offering them to her doctor as a gesture of gratitude. "Thank you!" The creature took the leaf, chittering something as she disappeared back into the crowd.

This was a food of abundance, but it was the gesture that counted. Lizzy leaned against Schaef, her attention already drawn back to the cliff carvings. "Do you think they'll let me climb around to get a better look?"

"Coming from the woman with leaf socks?" I gave Lizzy an 'are you serious' look, before turning back to Yinet. I held up my empty leaf, tapping my stomach. "Thank you." I set the leaf aside, turning my head back to the cliffs too. "This is home?"

Of course she didn't understand. Lizzy helped, pulling out her sketch pad and doing a quick drawing of our tents. I got her drift, point to them and to my own chest. "Home." I pointed to the cliffs and to her. "Home."

She grasped my meaning and pointed to the cliffs. "Hom." She pointed to us, then the cliffs again. "Hom."

Remy grasped her meaning as I did and leaned into our conversation. "Yes, thank you for bringing us to your home." He looked at me and shrugged. "Just saying. Anyway, it's been a rough day and it'll be dark soon. If we get a good night's rest we can spend tomorrow exploring this place." He looked to Lizzy. "Maybe your feet will be up to it by."

"I'm not about to miss a thing if I have to crawl around on my hands and knees." It was getting darker and she leaned her head against Schaeffer's shoulder again.

He wrapped his arm around her, jerking his head at me. "I guess you should find out where we can pitch tents for the night."

"Probably don't need to." I pointed at Lizzy and her feet, looking at Yinet and Gerret. "Home? Sleep." I rested my face against my hands, closing my eyes.

Yinet stared at me for a moment, then swept her hand to the cliffs. "Hom."

Gerret called out to the group and several scurried forward, grabbed our backpacks before running for the cliffs. They bounced up the cliff walls, disappearing into carved arches. We followed Yinet to find steps, large steps.

Lizzy was in no shape for climbing, so Remy and I went first, reaching back to help Schaeffer bring her up, until a large female appeared and offered her back to Lizzy, patting her shoulders repeatedly.

"Oh, I get it." Lizzy shrugged. "It's been a while, but it beats the alternative." Schaef helped her onto the LR's back. She laughed as she wrapped her arms and legs around the LR. It sounded like the LR laughed too.

Yinet gave me a cheek nuzzle. "Tomrow."

"Tomorrow. Thank you." I followed our guide up the terraced ledges. They were steep, but Remy offered me a hand up, since he didn't have to carry the packs.

We got a few chitters from the nearest LR when Schaeffer reached out for me too. I reminded him of the apparent custom, so he held his hand back until Remy touched me first. That seemed fine by them.

When we reached our terrace, Lizzy sat on a bench, watching the LR adjust and remoisten the leaves around her feet. She smiled. "I guess I just have to keep the wraps wet."

"Tomrow!" The LR bounced away and down the cliff, not using the terrace.

Lizzy leaned out as far as she dared. "Wow, I hope you're recording this."

"Every moment." I tapped the little recorder attached to my collar. Schaef had one too. We'll upload today's data." I looked to Schaef. "See if you have a signal up here and get in touch with base, let them know our status?"

"Soon as we get settled." He glanced below us, to the LR still watching us intently. "Right now we have an audience. You'd think they never saw a human before."

"Seeing and having us here are two whole different stories." I looked to the arches. "Well, let's see what we have for accommodations."

Inside the entrance we found our packs neatly lined up. I'd expected it to be dark, but there was some type of phosphorescent plant around the interior arch, sending tendrils out into the sunlight. The leaves glowed, stretching out across the cave's ceiling. "Wow, this gives a whole new definition to 'going green'."

I reached up to brush my hand over the leaves, only to pull it back quickly. Even the slightest touch seemed to shut down the process, the light going out in those leaves. Fortunately, they glowed back to life slowly. “Interesting.”

“Comfy too.” Remy beckoned me over to another archway. “All the comforts of home.” The room was clearly a sleeping chamber, a large flat shelf along the back wall. Large enough for two LR. It was covered with a layer of woven reeds and blankets.

“Ah, good, two bedrooms, and what appears to be a bath. Running water and all. You got to see this.” Schaef waved us deeper into the cavern.

We followed the trail of light as the plant’s tendrils fed from somewhere in the depths of the cave. We passed another sleep chamber and in the back of the cave, found the host plant as well as another chamber. Inside the room we found a channel cut into the wall.

Schaeffer reached up to a wooden handle, pulling it down. Water spouted down into a stone trough. He ran his hand through the water, then he scanned it. “Pure! I can take this as suitable for drinking, but it goes to another container.” Schaef pointed to a smaller arch to the side of the room. “They observe hygiene.”

Inside was a toilet, though a bit scary in size. Water from the sink was stored in another tank to be used to rinse down this basin. I laughed at the thought of being rescued from the hole cut in the floor. “Used worse, but I think we’d better set up our own. Good a place as any.”

“Yeah, Lizzy said as much.” Schaef laughed too, pushing us out of the facilities. “I’ll take care of it. If you want to get out some MREs, berries aren’t going to tide me over to morning.”

“Deal.”

We sorted out the food while Schaef set up the portable toilet. Though our environmental team said controlled disposal of waste would have no effect, we'd abide by regulations.

I laid out our sleeping bags over the reed mats and Remy activated our heat-n-eats. Lizzy grumbled at being dragged inside. She ate half her meal before nodding off. Schaef carried her to bed.

I wasn't so easily lulled, still flying too high from this discovery. Remy joined me on the terrace, letting his legs dangle over the edge, watching the LR end their day. No matter who I was, this was a once in a lifetime experience. Missing a single minute was criminal.

Below, the LR glanced up at us, but went about their business. "I'm not one of your xeno-guys, but I'd think with the size of their eyes they're more adapted to night vision than we are." Remy leaned back to stare up into the sky, at the first sparkle of stars.

I followed his gaze. The trees around the cliffs were sparse and one of the moons was already cresting the mountain edge. "Two moons should be out tonight, but yeah, won't see much without the goggles. Are you game for watching?"

"I'm game as long as you are, though it's been a long day." He wrapped his arm around me. We'll be here for a few days, I assume."

"Try to drag me back to camp."

CHAPTER THIRTEEN

Morning came with Lizzy shaking us out of our nest, excited and buzzing a mile a minute. “Wake up already. Geez, I’d think you’d have been up with the sun.” She dragged off our blankets, limping a bit yet as she dodged Remy.

I glanced at my watch, seeing it was well past dawn. “I guess I was more tired than I thought. You look much better.”

Lizzy flaunted her heels. “Miracle cure, though I think I’ll skip the boots for another day or two.” Typical civilian, she’d packed flip-flops. She bounced out the doorway. “Hurry up. The LR delivered breakfast.”

“Glad she’s better. Hate to leave her on the sidelines. We’d never hear the end of it.” Remy climbed off the ledge, grabbing up the blanket she’d pulled off. “Man, slept like a rock, which is surprising. You?”

I had to jump down from the bed. “It was a hell of a lot better than I thought, and certainly better than bags on the ground.” I straightened our area up, not wanting the LR to think we were slobs. Lizzy and Schaef waited on the terrace, breakfast laid out. Below the LR were up and about. From our vantage point we could see the organization of the village. We studied it over berries and some sort of melon.

Lizzy pointed out a group of youngsters, clustered together with several older LR. “I’m taking that as school. I’d love to sit in, see if I can sort it out. You know, kids are my specialty.”

“Let’s meet with Yinet and see what she has in mind for us. If there’s no objections, it’s fine with me.” I looked around, watching the flow of LR up and down the cliffs. Like in the forests, they easily leapt from one level to the next, except for a few of the citizens who used the terraces as we had. “This is so odd, so primitive, though they created this?”

“So did many of our own cultures.” Schaef gave me a ‘you should know’ glance.

I rolled my eyes at him. “It’s the first thing on my agenda, figuring this part of it out. I’m going to assume you’ll be working on the mountain itself?”

“It’s what brought us here.” He’d been more interested in it than the LR, running his hands over the rocky surfaces. “If we can reach some sort of deal…” He shook his head at my raised eyebrow. “Yeah, a deal. I concede. They’re fully sentient.” He let his eyes be pulled back up the cliffs. “Everything we know will change with this information.”

Remy shook his head too. “Only yesterday I thought we were limited to our little bitty solar system and today I’m here.” He waved his hand out over the village. “People would kill for this opportunity alone.”

“Which is a scary thought.”

Remy looked at me, confused.

“It was one thing when we had hopes of no sentient life forms here. Extraction would proceed by policy. Now we face a whole other set of rules. Greed can outweigh rules.”

"True… but I don't think it'll be an immediate concern." Remy looked perplexed, as he was trying to sound confident. "From what I picked up, you only have two functioning ships, which means a controlled extraction, if an agreement can be reached. It'll still take years before new ships come off the line. By then the Corps should have the process secure."

"Yeah, but look at history, at every major 'gold rush' scenario. Eventually the bad guys always show up." I was not so sure about the Alliance's ability to control the future. "By now our report on sentience has been transmitted, so they'll be shifting the plan."

Deep down I cringed. We needed the ore, but that hinged on communications. That was my game, Kazan's.

Despite conditioning, my Batista side was the one who'd come out enough to equate them with Zebra, enough to throw my brain into some mental short-out, maybe starting long before I returned home. At least that was the suspicion growing in my head as both sides found common ground. I tried not to resist them.

We finished our breakfast in silence, then climbed down from our vantage point. Lizzy's shoes plop-plopped behind us as we went in search of Yinet.

It took a while, but we found her up another cliff, in a circle of other females. They were chittering intensely and I got the distinct impression it was about us, from the frequent glances at us. Yinet came off strong, determined, definitely a leader. Figuring out the politics would be an important step too, so we didn't step on the wrong toes.

We waited quietly, observing without staring, letting our lapel cameras record the proceedings. Eventually the other females quietly dropped out of the circle, giving us a wide berth and disappearing along the cliffs.

Yinet took another moment, before extending her fingers in her beckoning fashion. "Ara. Litty." She didn't ask for our men. Maybe because Gerret wasn't with her. Remy and Schaef got the message, remaining on their rocks.

Lizzy couldn't resist as she got up to follow me, turning back to Schaeffer. "Now, you be good boys. Stay. Sttaay!"

"Lizzy!" She jumped and laughed at my snap, falling in behind me.

Yinet only cocked her head. We all had a lot to learn about each other. Lizzy's humor might not make the process easy. As I reached Yinet, I stuck out my face for the nuzzle. "Good morning." I made the sun gesture I'd worked on with them, showing it in the rising position.

"Gud morn!"

Lizzy giggled at Yinet's nuzzle, her fur tickling. "Good morning, Yinet."

I glanced back at Remy and Schaef, just as Gerret popped up the face of the terrace. He gestured to them to go with him. Schaef gave Remy the jerk of a head and they headed back down the face of the cliff. I turned back to Yinet. "I guess it's just us. Where to start…"

"Start with why we're here, total honesty." Lizzy smiled playfully, but spoke seriously.

"Way too much, too soon. I need to understand them better, like all this." I rolled my head back to look up the cliff, then reached my hand out to follow an artistic curl carved in the stone.

"It wasn't all done with chisels. Where's their technology. Did they do it themselves, or someone else, another species? Or did they just find it like this, a previous civilization." I pulled my hand away from the wall. Damn, now I was sounding like Schaeffer and his alien pyramid theories.

"That's a lot to pick apart at this stage." Lizzy reached out her hand to touch the wall too, but stared sharply at Yinet. "You…" With her other hand she waved to the village below the terrace. "You and your people did this?" She faced back to the stone, letting her fingers slip into a crevice, pretending to scoop it out. "You did this?"

Yinet studied her gestures for a moment. "Yettt." She stood up from her bench. "Cum." She held her hand upwards, pointing even higher up the cliff. "Tory."

I was willing to go wherever she wanted, but 'tory'. I played with the word a bit. "Tory?"

"Story, silly!" Lizzy grabbed my arm. "Remember, no 's' sounds. You told them stories, now she wants to tell us one."

That made sense, I started so many drawing sessions with 'I want to tell you a story'. Clearly Yinet had been putting my words together for some time.

"Story time." I gave our hostess a nod and she started up the cliff, walking, giving Lizzy a hand up. Flip-flops weren't ideal for the task, but probably better than blisters.

We climbed, higher and higher, all the way to the top terrace. There we entered another cavern, the ceiling covered with the plants that glow bright. She led us back into a long corridor.

Immediately I found my drawings, stuck to the wall. In one row were the stories I'd told about me and Lizzy. In another were also the drawings where I'd tried to describe our journey to and from their planet.

My cheeks felt hot as Lizzy laughed at my artwork. "I need to give you some lessons before you run into any other alien species."

"Hey, it got the message across enough for them to start talking to us."

Lizzy shrugged and went back to the art display.

Soon my pictures were replaced by others, older, carved into the stone. Carved with a precision that excluded any chisel. I ran my fingers along the lines, feeling the sharp edges, no nicks, hesitation notches or irregularities. “Wow. How’d they do this?”

“How, might not be the question you want to ask.”

CHAPTER FOURTEEN

Lizzy stood in front of another wall, staring at a mural. I backed up, taking in more of the carvings. It took a second before I realized what mesmerized her.

I saw the mountain, the beautiful face so intricate in smaller detail, but it was only one of many carvings on the wall, interconnected drawings.

I followed Lizzy as she took a step deeper into the artwork. The next image was of the same mountain, but no city cut into its face.

Next came a city almost like our own, but it wasn't pretty. It wasn't artistic like the cliffs. It was broken, destroyed, and from it came a flood of creatures, led by what had to be the LR.

In three simple carvings, I'd learned these people came from a higher civilization, but I could see more carvings. I started back through history, standing before each panel to take it in, to understand what I saw and to record it in as much detail as I could.

Lizzy was at my side, staying close and quiet. Yinet also made no sounds, offering no explanation. This wall needed no words. Art was our common language.

By the time we reached the last of the carvings, I needed air. I needed the light of a real sky. We made the terrace and sat down on the long benches. Yinet sat down across from me, staring at me. She was waiting.

"I don't know what to say. Your people have been through so much, and survived. Now we're here to upset everything."

Lizzy leaned on my shoulder. "I don't think she wants us to be sad. I think she put your drawings in there for a reason. Did you notice how the ones of how we got here follow their lives? The others were placed above or below those, while our travel was in direct line. We're part of their history now. They see us in themselves, at least I did."

So did I. At one point in the drawings, ships lifted off their world, up beyond their atmosphere. "Is that why you were curious about us? Because your people once went out there?"

She scowled at my hand signals, so I repeated myself, slower. She gestured going out, but waved off coming back, pointing to us instead. She made several more gestures, playing with words. "Ara tee LR?" She turned her eyes outward.

"Did I 'see' LR out there?" I repeated the question and she nodded. All I could do was shake my head. "No, but out there is so big, so far, and we are so small." I did my best to translate the thoughts, but only got a frown from Yinet.

Lizzy did better than I did, but she was accustomed to communicating larger ideas down to the simplest explanations.

I sat back as Lizzy cleared a space on the terrace, then from a nearby bush she plucked a hand full of leaves and a couple small twigs. She pulled one large leaf from her pile and put it on the ground between us. "Home… Hippotigris…"

"Don't use that name, it was a bad joke."

"Okaay… LR world. LR home." She slapped the leaf, then held up one small leaf. "Star."

"Tar." Yinet knew that word, pointing to the sky and giving the sign for night.

With a flourish, Lizzy scattered the tiny leaves across the stone, around the larger leaf. "Many stars." She took one twig and pretended to fly a space ship up and away from the planet, just as the picture had shown. "LR go to the stars."

From another direction she flew in the other twig. "Here come the crazy humans." She made a few stops at stars along the way, shaking her head and lifting off again, until she came to the large leaf. "And here we are. Human and LR."

She went back to the LR stick, stopping at one star, then another, and another, but going further away, and not in the direction we came from. She went through them going away, our coming here and Yinet got it, nodding. "Many tar, go far."

Lizzy went over to sit beside Yinet. "Too many stars."

Yinet didn't say anything for a minute or two. Finally she reached down to take the 'human' twig. "Human." She broke the stick into two pieces and pointed one at me. "Ara." She pointed out to the forest, the way we'd come the day before. "Ara." She put the stick back on the leaf, pointing towards our camp.

She held out the other stick. "Human." She said in in a lower voice and stared at me for another second, then pointed off towards distant mountains. She growled and put the other stick on the leaf, harder. "Many human."

"What? No. No more humans!" I shook my head and started to reach for the stick, but Yinet's long fingers wrapped around my wrist, stopping me. "Yinet. No more humans." I pointed back in the direction of our camp. "Only in camp and here."

"No. Many human." She pointed again in the direction she had before. With her hand curled, she pretended to dig, growling. "Many human."

"That's not possible!" I looked out in the direction she pointed. She had no reason to lie, so what could she be talking about. "I don't understand."

I reached for the second stick again, and this time she let me pick it up. "Many human, over there, digging." I picked up a nearby rock and held it out, then put it in my pocket. "Taking rock?"

Her head nodded.

"LR over there? LR village over there?" I pointed to her, to the face of their dwellings, then pointed in the same direction as she had.

"No LR." She pointed further south. "LR hom." Then to another mountain. "LR hom." Whatever was happening was a distance between two more of these peoples' villages, but close enough they knew about it.

She pointed down over the face of the cliff, down to the terrace where we'd joined her. "LR…" She growled something in her language. She repeated herself, but when I still didn't understand the word, she lunged her head forward, baring her teeth, then quickly pulled back, returning to her usual calm expression.

It was terrifying. "Okay… Mad, ang… the LR are angry."

My stomach flipped over at the thought. "Those other females. Tribal leaders. Came here to be angry, at us." Lizzy translated with drawings. Yinet nodded. "Damn!" I tapped at my lapel. "Schaeffer, where are you?"

What if they brought us here for a reason? That was stupid. Of course they did. But they'd waited for me. Why?

"Schaeffer here, what's wrong?"

"Where the hell are you, right now?"

"Getting a tour of the village. It wraps around the western ridge. There's got to be thousands of LR here." He sounded fascinated. "What's got you all freaked out?"

"You tell me. Other than our camp, how many other humans are here, and why didn't I know anything about it."

"Because there aren't. We're the only ones here." Now annoyed was the prevailing tone in his voice. "We got people in orbit."

"No, we also got people at…" I used my scanner to get a reading on the distant mountains, even if I couldn't pinpoint exactly where. "…150 degrees to the south. The LR aren't happy about this, not one bit. Though it seems they still trust me to answer them. So, tell me again, why do we have another camp and why are they mining without permission."

"Listen Kazan. I already told you. We don't have anyone else here." He paused. "We're heading back your way. We'll contact the ship and get them to do a scan. If you don't like that answer, we'll take the shuttle over to find out for ourselves. Deal?"

"Deal." I turned down the pissed off dial. He wouldn't compromise if he was pulling something, and I'd worked with him long enough to know when he was telling me the truth. But so was Yinet.

When I turned around, Lizzy had been busy, doing her interpreting of my argument and the plan. It seemed to placate Yinet. It also brought on a wave of jealousy as Yinet gave her a nuzzle. I'd spent countless months of my life here, hiding what I was from my dearest, and in a matter of two days she'd gotten just as far.

I sighed out the unexpected jealously, not knowing which of my personalities let it out in the first place. I focused until I had Kazan front and center again. We had a mission here. If Lizzy could talk to them better than me, good. I needed to be using my head for other things, like figuring out what the fuck was going on, and who was doing it.

“Okay, we’re going to get to the bottom of this. Maybe it’s a misunderstanding. Maybe a survey team got over-zealous.”

“Maybe we got bad guys already.”

“Maybe you better not translate that. Let’s get off this cliff and find out what we can.”

Lizzy followed me to the steps. Yinet led the way, helping us down the huge steps, almost making it a game with Lizzy, swinging her down from one step and over the next to the ledge below.

To not be the stick in the mud, I played along, even had a bit of fun before we hit our terrace. Schaef and Remy were waiting.

Schaeffer wasted no time. “I called the ship’s captain. She said our other ship is a thousand light-years off in the other direction. She’s running an EM scan, but you know as well as I do, we only have these two ships.”

“That you know about.” Remy chirped in. “Remember where the science came from, private industry. They wouldn’t let something this major get past them.”

Remy had a point, though neither of us wanted to hear it. Schaeffer scowled. “Nothing’s impossible, so we need to address the likelihood that either the Corps or the corporations are scamming the LR, and head it off before they get really pissed off.”

“Yeah…” I looked up at Yinet. “You really don’t want to see what an angry LR looks like. Not so warm and fuzzy.”

CHAPTER FIFTEEN

"Can we fix one thing before we go any further?" Lizzy still had an arm wrapped over Yinet's, like they were now best buds.

I squashed down another wave of jealousy, Batista's jealousy. As much as she loved her friend like a sister, Lizzy always had a knack for becoming the center of attention among their friends. Kazan knew it was a benefit here. "Fix away."

"They have a name. Calling them LR is like calling them It." She glanced up at Yinet. "Pa-re-dat." She said it slowly.

"Par-red-et." Yinet rolled the r's, a half-growling sound, the last syllable sharp.

I repeated it precisely, getting what passed as Yinet's smile. "Parredet. Sorry if I offended." I bowed my head to her. "I should have asked as soon as we started talking."

"Well, Babe, not like you run into aliens every day. At least not yet." Remy wrapped his arm around my shoulders. "Let's get details, how you came by your info."

Thanks to the lapel cameras, we replayed the scene from the art gallery, wowing our men who'd been deprived of the private showing. Schaeffer was pissed off, but kept it hidden, even as I told him of the Parredet once achieving space travel.

But it was Yinet asking about the ‘other humans’ digging up the far mountain that broke Schaeffer’s calm. He pulled up a topographical map of where we were, our camp and the mountains.

Yinet liked the holographic technology, not the least bit afraid of it. Rather, she located her village without his help. She ran her long finger through the mountain range, over several peaks, to a precise target.

Armed with specific coordinates, Schaeffer passed them along to the captain, and again we waited. It seemed to take an eternity, but soon enough she came back on-line. “Col. Schaeffer, we did a full sweep of the area and got some unusual readings.”

“You’re picking up activity? Human activity?”

“We’re picking up something we shouldn’t be, a lot of scanner interference. I have my guys working to get a better reading.” Funny how distance did little to distort her underlying message. She didn’t like being jammed.

“Well, if you can’t get a specific answer with your scanners, send us a shuttle and we’ll go take a look.” Schaeffer snipped.

“Sorry, I won’t authorize that. Not yet.”

“What?”

I cringed. The pissing match was about to start.

“Sir, we don’t know what’s down there. Do you really want to risk a fly-by, unprepared, unarmed?” She hesitated on her end, making him think about it. “Give us time to see if we can break through these wacked out signals. If we can’t get detailed scans by the end of the day, I’ll put together an armed detail and send the shuttle to you.”

Lizzy started translating. I almost stopped her, but Yinet’s trust was important. We had to be totally honest with her. Which meant telling her why we were here. "Yinet?" I pulled the rock out of my pocket, holding it out to her, giving it back. "Let us talk more."

Lizzy had to get out her sketchpad to explain why we came here. Yinet remained quiet for such a long time. We had come here for the specific reason of taking away the ore, to build more ships. The difference was our intentions. Our mission statement was clear we wouldn't take resources if the planet's life forms were sentient.

The Parredet changed the plan. My new mission was to negotiate any possible trade agreement. Unfortunately, someone violated the plan before I could even start. I promised we would make them stop.

I waited, sitting easily within reach of Yinet's long arms, and teeth. I had to be honest and vulnerable, if she was to believe in me.

It took a long time, but finally she bowed her head to us. "Ara, friend. Litty, friend." She said the words, but we didn't get the nuzzle, making my chest ache. "Parredet talk."

She got up and left. Lizzy let out her breath. "She's not happy, but she'll stand by us."

"Glad you're confident." Schaeffer came to the bench. "I don't like waiting for answers."

Remy stood at the terrace edge, watching Yinet leave "I'm sure they didn't either, but they spent as much time studying us as you spent trying to figure them out. They wanted Shara to come back, to reveal themselves to her, to confront her. We have to rely on that trust."

"I don't think it's their trust we have to worry about." Lizzy tucked her pad back into her bag. "What if the scans confirm there's some illegal mining operation going on? How are we going to stop them?"

Remy turned back from the ledge. “She’s right. That ship up there isn’t a battle cruiser. You didn’t build it for that purpose. I doubt we can say the same for these others, whoever they are.” Remy stared at Schaeffer. “They came here with the specific purpose of taking what they wanted, and to hell with anyone getting in their way. You think they’ll stop, because you tell them to?”

“No, I don’t think that. Not at all.” Schaeffer looked out over the mountains.

“I’m sick just thinking about all this.” I pushed off the bench, past Remy and into the cavern. “I need to think. Let me know when we hear from the captain.”

I left them on the ledge, grabbed an MRE and headed to the sleeping chamber. I crawled deep into the ledge, away from the lighted leaves covering the ceiling, back where it was cool and dark. There I pulled out the cookies and nibbled on them, thinking about all I’d done here, since day one. All my work, undermined.

What would happen if some LR… some Parredet approached these outlaws. This could get ugly, quick, and we were light-years from home. All the firm resolve I’d put out for Yinet dissolved and I curled up under the blanket.

“Are you sulking?” Remy crawled up next to me, pulling at the blanket, the Parredet blanket, so delicate looking, but strong fibers holding up as he tried to see my face.

“No, I’m thinking how screwed we are. You know I have to go dark before I can start thinking about how to fix this mess.” It was a habit both Kazan and Batista shared.

Of course, Remy never respected it. I gave up trying to keep my face covered as he came up under the blanket too.

“We’re soldiers. We were trained as soldiers, before we went off into our separate specialties. We’re going to have to be soldiers again. We can recall our sister-ship, pack it with real soldiers and get their asses here to confront these people."

"Yes…" Remy hesitated. "If you're going to the dark scenarios, consider whether or not your command is behind this."

I looked over at him. "You would bring that up.

"You know me. Devil's advocate."

"I'm sorry I got you into this. You and Lizzy."

"I'd rather be here than you going through this without my even knowing." He kissed me. "We're in this together, remember? You, me and Kazan. No more secrets"

"I remember." I curled up close to him, glad he'd come to join my sulking. "I can't believe they're doing this, virtually under our noses. What are they, less than two hundred miles away? Maybe if I hadn't been playing secret agent, I'd have found out about this sooner."

"You can't blame yourself for this, part-time or full-time, you were doing your job the way you were instructed. I'm sure if command were in on this, they wouldn't have been so demanding about you figuring out the local life. We have to keep faith in that part of the mission, though I wouldn't guarantee all levels of command have clean hands."

"Really? Why do you think that?"

"Someone told them about this place, in order to get smugglers here."

I pulled the blanket down so I could look at him. "Since when are you the one to go down all these conspiracy paths?"

"Who reads all the political mysteries? Beats the crap you read." His hands slipped down my back. "All those sappy romances. At least when you're Batista. I don't know this Kazan person so well yet. What do you read when you're out here?"

“What do you think? Science-fiction, of course.” I laughed as his hands pulled me tighter. “I’m getting the impression you’d go for a bit of sappy romance.”

“Really?” Remy pinned me down for a kiss. “Why would you be getting that impression?” His hand pressed between us, unfastening my belt. “I certainly wouldn’t want to mislead you. I’m just trying to help clear your head.”

“We’re not alone. Schaef and Lizzy...”

“Went for a walk.” Remy sat up and removed his shirt. “A nice long walk.”

CHAPTER SIXTEEN

The Parredet went about their business as we waited for the captain to get back to us on her scans. Lizzy took the time to download the history lesson we'd gotten and put in narration, as best as we could without an accurate translation from Yinet.

Schaeffer and Remy studied our morning log, catching up on details they'd missed. Any doubt as to Yinet's meaning was erased, not that Schaeffer doubted me. It was mid-afternoon when Schaeffer's comm chirped at him impatiently.

"Schaeffer here. What do you have for us?" He turned the volume up for us all to hear.

"We need to send the shuttle for you. The jamming is intentional, which means they know we're here. I've put together an armed detail to provide protection at the camp until we can get our people aboard."

I'd heard that tone in the captain's voice. She was on full alert, ready to make a run for it as soon as everyone was safe. I tapped into the link. "I'm sorry, Captain, but we're not going to abandon these people. We brought this on them."

"Col. Kazan, you don't know that." She was about to order us back.

"Yes, we do. The Parredet are perfectly clear we arrived first, then this other batch of humans showed up. The fact we tried to make contact with them is why they trust us. They trust we'll take care of this problem."

I looked around at my small party. We'd spent the day conjecturing on how this other faction learned of this world. "They didn't go hopping randomly to every faint molecular signal. They sat back prepping their resources. We found it and someone in the organization leaked the info to them."

The other end was silent for a moment. No doubt she'd already run through a few conspiracy theories herself. "Either way, you're not safe down there."

"We're as safe here as back at camp." Schaeffer pulled the link back. "Send me a shuttle. Make it absolutely clear that the indigenous life-forms are NOT the enemy. I want no instances of hostilities towards them, no matter what they do. At this point they consider us allies."

"Schaef, what are you planning?" I leaned across, whispering.

He waved me off. "Pick me up in one hour. I'll send coordinates."

Clear of the connection, he got up from our circle. "I need to get aboard the ship to report back to HQ, to get our sister ship remissioned."

Lizzy bit at her lip, looking up at him. "You're coming back?"

It was an odd question, sounding a bit worried. Schaef gave her a strange gaze back. "Of course." He smiled at her. "You'll be safe here. You just keep working with Yinet on their history and culture. We want as much detail as possible."

I got up too, waving to Yinet and pointing to include Gerret. They started up the cliff. “An hour. You’re intending to be picked up somewhere else?”

Schaef looked to the distant range. Its height made it visible, even from our vantage point. “They’ll be watching to see if we know about them yet. If I can hitch a ride further down the range, we can keep them from pinpointing this location. We don’t know how well the Parredet have been hiding from them, hopefully a lot better than they did from us.”

“I’ll try to get it across to Yinet for the other villages to lay low, and that we might have to wait for backup. They’ve waited this long to tell us…trust us. Hopefully we can keep this contained.” I stepped back as Gerret crested the ridge first. Yinet came up beside him. She gave me a nuzzle before going to Lizzy. Her mood had improved.

I waited until they both perched on the benches to try explaining what we wanted to do. Lizzy was going fast and furious to draw it out, to make it as clear as possible.

Yinet studied the plan for a moment, then studied me, as if trying to read my mind, my intentions. Turning to Gerret, she rambled out a long series of their chirping communications. He gave her a quick nuzzle before disappearing down the cliff face.

“I take that as a go?” Schaef picked up his pack, but stopped as Yinet gave him a curious look. He held the pack for a moment, before handing it to Lizzy. “I probably won’t need this and it’s just more weight to carry.”

“Leaving it indicates you’ll return.” Lizzy took it, putting it behind her. “However, she probably expects a ‘see you later’.” She stuck her face out to Schaeffer.

Seeing him blush was weird. As weird as him bending down to give Lizzy a kiss. “That good for you?”

"Had better." Lizzy smirked. "But I'll wait for you to come back."

Gerret returned with two large Parredet. They remained on the edge of the cliff wall as their leader spoke to them, gesturing to the southeast. He knew a location suitable for the shuttle to land, but far enough away to be misleading. He motioned for Schaef to approach.

Though this was his idea, I could see Schaef pale just a little. Lizzy saw it also, going to him and giving him another kiss and nuzzle, as our hosts would. "Just hang on and think about being eight years old. They'll do all the work."

"You'd know?" He turned to the first of the two giant males.

"I went to circus camp for book research." Lizzy gave him a push, laughing as the first male grabbed Schaef and swung him around onto the other male's back. Schaef scrambled to get a grip, before falling down the side of the cliff. "Remember to let go when they do." She shouted her instructions down the wall as the two males disappeared, two more joining them as they reached the trees.

I watched too, gritting my teeth. "Man, he's going to hate me when he gets back."

"It was his idea." Lizzy still giggled. Yinet did too.

I backed away from the edge. "Let's get to the rest of the message, so Yinet can get her emissaries on their way too."

Hearing her name, Yinet rejoined me on the bench, Lizzy next to her with the drawing pad. I talked, Lizzy sketched and Yinet gave me slow head nods, mimicking our gestures. When I got out the last of my instructions, she gave us nuzzles and disappeared over the cliff.

Remy had sat by quietly throughout our exchanges. He looked a bit dejected. "What's wrong, Hon?"

"Just feeling left out, I guess." He came over to take Yinet's vacant spot. "Nothing to build or fix, and no boy scout duties right now."

"Sorry. Maybe you should have gone with Schaef."

"No, he'd want me here, just in case." Remy gave Lizzy an elbow. "He'd worry you'd get yourself in some kind of trouble."

"With who?" Lizzy nudged him back. "Let's see about that tour you two were getting. We've only seen the history cave and there's so much to learn yet." She saw me look down at her feet and she kicked one out. "I'm much better, really."

The raw blisters had dried up and there was only a slight redness to them. "Our medics would be interested in those leaves."

"Again, your field, not mine." Remy stood up, offering Lizzy a hand, even though she didn't need it. "Come on, I'll show you as much as we saw, then hopefully we'll find someone you can talk to about the rest."

Lizzy took his hand, but let go quickly, nodding to the Parredet village. It was pushing customs to be in close proximity while Schaeffer was away, best not to outright break them intentionally. He went down the terrace, giving us each a hand down, me first. We both helped Lizzy, until a female arrived to accompany her, proving the Parredet were keeping tabs on us.

At the base of the cliff, the female stayed with us, but dropped back a discreet distance as we walked through the village commons studying the cliff carvings. Lizzy was the artist among us, but after a few minutes I could see a flow, a pattern, far more intricate than the cave. We followed as much as we could from the ground. As we moved further from our point of residence, the carvings changed. There seemed to be breaks, like turning pages.

“Eras. What we saw was an abbreviated version.” Lizzy held her arms out to encompass the current cliff face. “This section is an entire era.” She stepped back. “They recorded every moment of their history, documented for the next generations, to never be forgotten.” She looked further down the range. “Somewhere we’ll be added.”

“Let’s hope it’s a good annotation.” I’d joined her as she’d moved back far enough to look up the cliff a bit more easily. “So, the cave, why that, if they have all this?”

“Book blurbs.” Lizzy looked at me. “We grasped the truth faster in those few feet, than we did looking at thousands of feet.” She spread her arms out. “Now you’re prepared to read the whole book and believe.”

“You mean comic strip vs. War and Peace.” Remy turned away from us. “This goes on and on, virtually the whole mountain.”

“I believe, but never expected anything like this. We need to go back to the beginning, record as much as possible and figure these people out. There’s so much we need to know, like where they used to live. Why they rejected all their technology to live like this.” I looked around, at our escort. “Why a clearly intelligent species had chosen to continue living like this.”

“Don’t criticize.” Lizzy snapped at me. “If these people faced a catastrophic history, this is their answer, to return to nature.” Lizzy drew as she spoke, something she’d done since she was a kid, probably what made her such a good writer, being able to split her thoughts so completely.

“I wasn’t criticizing.” I hadn’t meant to. “I’m worried.”

Lizzy looked up at me. “So am I.”

What was about to happen on this peaceful planet was terrifying. “Let’s get everything we can.”

Lizzy was quick to get the female to understand what we wanted. Getting to the beginning of the story was far more difficult. We found out just how large this village was. We did as much as we could, returning at nightfall.

We barely had MREs out of our packs when Schaeffer slipped off the back of a Parredet, with a great deal more ease than he'd left. He bowed to the gentle giant before turning to us. "It's not our people over there. I got word out to reroute our other ship, with soldiers."

"And in the meantime?" His arrival took me off guard. Our new friends never even raised an alarm at his return. At least any I heard. Yinet knew, showing up only a bare second after Schaef.

He gave Yinet a bow, then Lizzy a proper smooch, as a mate should.

"What's the plan?" Formalities grated on my Kazan nerves, considering what was going on behind our backs.

Schaeffer sat down with Lizzy, switching back to the serious officer I knew. "We need to send a scouting party out to see exactly what's going on over there. I brought back some… tools." He looked up as Gerret joined our group. "As the Parredet are skilled at moving about quietly, we need to enlist their help in this. A party of soldiers with Parredet escorts."

Lizzy was quick to know her role, drawing out a quick sketch. Gerret nodded.

"I'll take a party of males back to our camp to get soldiers. Four. I don't want so many as to make it impossible to maintain stealth."

"Four, with us that makes eight, and twice as many Par..."

"We're not going." Lizzy interrupted Remy, getting a glare I'd only seen him use a few times in our years together.

Schaeffer nodded. "Four soldiers and me. The rest of you remain here."

“Wait a minute. I’m no slacker.” Remy riled. “You want to see what they’re doing. I’m an engineer. I can tell you what they have for equipment.”

Schaeffer turned his glare to Remy. “No. If they see us, they’ll aim to kill. I want to get in and get out. You can identify equipment from the vids.”

Remy fumed at being rejected, at being left on the sidelines. That wasn’t conducive to his personality.

Unfortunately I agreed with Schaef. “If I stay, you stay.”

CHAPTER SEVENTEEN

The recall of our sister ship was approved. It would be restocked and armed, but would take two weeks for them to arrive. In the meantime we had to act as if we didn't know the other camp existed and hope the spy didn't get wind of our plan.

The Parredet helped us maintain surveillance on the enemy, sending data on the mining operation for Remy to analyze. Our soldiers were brought into the forest, as close to enemy territory as possible, then paired up with Parredet to help them trek the rest of the way in.

Schaeffer handled the soldiers while I played diplomat, schmoozing the matriarchal village leaders. Clan Mothers, as Lizzy corrected me often. She and Yinet were virtually inseparable as Lizzy worked to translate their history and culture, discovering children's sign language a great tool. The writer in her was in heaven.

I kept Batista's bouts of jealousy in check, not letting her out until the end of the day, when Remy and I were finally alone.

Two weeks seemed like forever, but it took that long to set up our invasion of the mining camp. The soldiers from the sister ship would be shuttled downside once the assault was ready to start, creating extra confusion for the miners.

As we transferred to the front line, I felt the war between my two sides surfacing. Outside of boot camp, Batista had no assault training. Kazan had trained extensively from the beginning, the Corps never sure what they'd run into as we explored outside our own solar system.

Even so, I'd never used the training, until now and had Remy and Lizzy to worry about. I also had the Parredet to worry about, creatures who'd shorn their warring ways, and we'd brought that poison back to their world. I looked at Yinet and Gerret, regretting ever coming here.

They'd joined us on the shuttle ride, but were no more amazed by it than the rest of our technology. The pilot flew up a ravine, staying below the ridge to reach the advance team's camp. Here our team would split up.

Lizzy stayed at Yinet's side, since she was the best at communications. Yinet's English had improved massively and her tribe had picked up many of the essential words the soldiers needed. But there were still moments that needed translations.

When we reached the clearing the shuttle team started setting up our command post. The rest of us were matched up with Parredet who would take us to the front lines. I worried about stealth, how quiet we could be, but our friends lived this life. The dropped us far enough from the forest edge to not be seen or heard.

Remy and I walked the last few meters, dropping into a crouch as we reached the ridge overlooking the mining camp. All the vids hadn't done the operation justice.

They'd maintained the trees about the mountain face, but rubble and trash was strewn about the floor of the forest. This particularly angered the Parredet. These men didn't respect any species. The bones of wildlife were strewn into the garbage piled at the forest's edge.

Remy slipped back behind the rock we'd been spying from. "Filthy animals. I'm ashamed of being in the same species."

"They've always been around." I joined him, ignoring the rock pressing between my shoulder blades. "What did you see of any significance?"

Remy pulled his thoughts back to the assignment. "Their equipment is vulnerable. We can take it out easily enough, but we'll need to get to their shuttle. I need a closer look." He crawled back into the foliage, before standing up again. I was on his heels.

Under the shade of the trees, our escorts waited. Remy pointed where he wanted to go and they grabbed us up for the treetop tour. It had taken nearly a day for me to dare to open my eyes and watch, but now I couldn't take my eyes off of the vantage point they gave us. I clung easily, aided by a harness the Parredet fashioned for us.

Our escorts carried us deeper into the forest to avoid detection. When we reached the other side of the valley, the Parredet cautiously dropped down to a ledge across from the miner's shuttle. They dissolved back into the forest and let us do our surveillance work.

Remy wriggled between two boulders, giving him a perfect vantage point. His quietness made me uneasy. I was about to prod him when he slipped back out of the boulders.

I didn't like the look on his face. "Well?"

"They're virtually the same design as our shuttles, right down to the rivet placement." He shook his head. "That confirms an inside job. Someone passed them the plans."

I wanted to crawl out for a look myself, but we were taking a chance as it was. "Let's get back to command. Schaeffer needs this info out on the next comm-link."

Remy crawled behind me, back to where we'd been dropped. Our escorts showed up, taking us back to our command post. Remy didn't speak at all, not until Schaeffer returned from his own reconnaissance. Campfires were out of the question, but we gathered around our food storage unit. He got his meal and quietly ate with Lizzy.

No one talked until we dropped our containers into recycling. Schaeffer leaned forward, setting his comm on the food box. "Let's get this over with. The link will be open for only a few seconds in the morning, so I have to have this coded and ready to go."

Each team leader reported in until it was our turn. Remy downloaded his surveillance vid, bringing up the mining equipment. "First, this will be the easy part. We can wreck it with just a few carefully placed explosives. Pop some charges along this shaft and it'll never be repairable." He ran his finger along the display, a line transmitted to everyone else's coms.

It was as simple as he'd claimed, but it was more than dismantling their mining equipment. The men in their camp looked rough and were armed. That added to the challenge of capturing as many of these men as possible, and finding out who hired them.

From equipment, Remy went to the shuttle. A projection appeared on everyone's screens and I could see why he'd been so quiet. "This is our largest threat." Their shuttle was identical to ours, except for the weapons.

Remy zoomed in on the engine exhausts. "This would be the ideal spot to disable their ship from flight, but we need to take out the weaponry. I'm an engineer, but without a better look, I can't tell you how to best destroy them. We need to take them out before we can bring in the second wave."

“Our recon should have caught this.” Schaeffer tapped at the weapons mounted on the upper half of the craft, enlarging the image.

“Maybe, but we had to get up close to see the modification.” I interrupted before he turned to the recon leader. “They were under orders to keep back a distance. We were close enough to throw rocks and hit it.”

Schaeffer gave me a nod. “A wise choice. It does confirms what recon observed. There’s no one manning the shuttle. If they’re that lax on security, we should send a team to secure it.”

“Better than destroying it.” Remy seemed to relax next to me. As an engineer, any plan to destroy the machine probably grated on his nerves.

I only gave him a glance, focusing on the mission, not Batista’s whispering in my head. “What about their mother ship? Any word on it?”

“Our probes haven’t detected any other ships. It may be they time their passage to avoid us. They come in, load what ore they can and take off again. So, we might have just missed them.” Schaef nodded.

“Then they’re not due back for weeks. Unless they know we called in our sister ship.”

“If they know, they haven’t notified these guys. I see no change in their operations.” Schaef faced the group, getting no more input. “Tomorrow we send our reports on the lowest broadcast range possible, then it’s a go.”

One of the officers pointed out several men. “We’ll take the shuttle.”

Schaef nodded, pleased this group seemed on top of the action. He stood up. “Hit the sack. I need you all on your top game in the morning.” He waited until all the other team leaders left, looking at me. “You too.”

⌘ ⌘ ⌘

Morning came with a knot of apprehension that Lizzy's mother would say was premonition. I hoped it wasn't, suiting up in full military battle gear. Remy sat by the fire when I came out of the tent. He had on full battle gear too.

"What are you doing?" I walked up and flipped the open epaulet. "You don't need all this. Not here."

Remy looked up at me. "If I was staying here."

"You are!" Both my personalities stepped up. "There's a big difference between basic training and assault training. Schaef!"

Remy stood up, blocking my path. "I'm going! Someone needs to be on the shuttle team who can decipher what those weapons do and figure out any changes in the original design."

"Yes. We do." Schaeffer stepped out of our shuttle, slinging a laser rifle over his shoulder. "Either we have someone who can instantly unscramble engines from weapons, or we destroy the shuttle."

"Then destroy it." I had to step around Remy. "This was never part of the deal."

"It was!" Remy pulled me back around. "I joined the same Alliance you did, accepting the same risks you did. There were no guarantees we'd serve it all in peacetime, never having to defend our oaths." He jerked his thumb to the rest of the teams. "I have a job to do and I'm going to do it."

Batista raged inside me, while my Kazan half stepped back. He was right. Schaeffer said nothing, already knowing what was probably going on in my head. "Yes, you do." Batista kept screaming at me. "I know you know this, but follow your team leader's orders, to the letter. If you get hurt, I'll kill you myself."

Remy didn't smile, but pulled me back towards him. "I'll be careful." He gave me a quick kiss, slinging his rifle over his shoulder. "You be careful too. This is for real."

"I know." I reached up and fastened the epaulet to secure the rifle strap for his trek through the forest. Off to the side, Lizzy had a look of apprehension to match my insides. To my other side was his team, waiting. "You better go."

Remy marched off with his team, greeted on the edge of the clearing by the Parredet. In seconds, they were gone.

Schaef was also readying his team to move out. I wanted to slap him, or was that Batista. I rubbed my forehead. Maybe this was reaching full integration, not knowing whose emotions were whose.

Just in case, I gave Batista a push back into the recesses of my mind. The last thing I needed was emotional distractions. I joined my team.

It wasn't the job I picked, but dictated by Parredet. I was the equivalent of Yinet in their eyes, the leader of the humans. I could go no further than the perimeter line. As leader, I had to remain a step up, a step outside of battle in order to see the entire picture.

At least that was how Lizzy explained it. All our women soldiers, who had earned their positions, were assigned to perimeter teams, leaving the invasion to 'the men'. Not that we wouldn't see action.

Once the assault began, the miners and security would seek cover in the forest, where we 'women' would be waiting. Except for Lizzy, thankfully.

She remained at the command post with Yinet, waiting to help where ever needed as wounded were brought in to be triaged. There would be wounded and in the end we all had one job, to defend the Parredet.

CHAPTER EIGHTEEN

Schaeffer broadcast the order.

From the tree line, our soldiers flooded out into the camp. The surprise attack worked. Miners fumbled about, confused to see Alliance bearing down on them. The ones with their wits about them pulled weapons, too slowly for the snipers in my group. They fell where they stood.

Some tried to make a run for the forest, but were tripped up by the debris they'd so carelessly tossed aside. If they made it into the trees, and past my line, the Parredet would be waiting for them. The assault was on.

From my vantage point, I could see the entire field. The miners who didn't run looked for leadership. I followed their searching glances, seeing a cluster of armed men by the drill. They used the massive tires as shields. "Schaef! Under the drill. Expect fire from that location. Whoever's in charge is there."

"Confirmed!" Schaeffer waved a team around to a position to get a bead on them. At the same time I set snipers on them. I let myself look towards the shuttle. We couldn't bring in our shuttles until we captured or destroyed theirs.

The third team's advance party charged the plateau, reaching the shuttle with no resistance. The rear access was open wide, not a miner or security person close enough to stop them. They gave the signal for the second half of the team to rush the shuttle.

From the drill I could see them realize they were about to lose their shuttle. One man viciously waved his arms and two security men made a run for the ramp carved in rock from the valley to the plateau. "Team Three! A couple armed security coming up. Snipers, take them out!"

"Yes, ma'am!" I got multiple responses and saw the two security dodging the hail of bullets and laser fire coming their way now. One went down, the other jumped to the valley again and gained cover.

The one who'd sent them shoved another man from the protection of the drill's massive body. He made it to the far side, hiding behind another tire. I passed the information to Schaeffer and our line to work around to his position.

I looked back to the shuttle as the other half of the team appeared at the edge of the forest and made a dash for the shuttle. I saw the first of our men hit. He staggered, but recovered.

"Where'd that come from?" I swung around to the various trajectories and saw two men on the other side of the valley, what must have been their perimeter security. "Snipers, Southeast..." I passed on the reading from my visor. Immediately we returned fire, trying to provide cover as the team made the shuttle.

I could see Remy, inside a knot of soldiers. The security detail didn't let up, even under combined fire. Remy jerked and fell.

"NO!" I started to lunge forward, through the perimeter, but my liaison officer drew me back. I struggled against her grip, looking to Remy. "REMY! Report."

Two soldiers grabbed him by the arms, towing him up the ramp while the rest of them closed ranks.

"REMY! REMY!"

"Col. Kazan!" The liaison officer jerked me around. "Kazan! Col. Schaeffer reminds you of battle protocol. Maintain open channels."

"Let go of me!" I jerked loose. "I know protocol."

"Col. Kazan! This is Team Three. Batista says to chill!"

It was what he'd say, relieving me slightly. "Fine. Secure that shuttle. Kazan out!" Knowing they had him, I returned my focus on the battle. As hard as our first line tried to keep the miners contained, the purpose of our second line was tested.

From my higher vantage point we passed on the coordinates of weak points in our line. Orders were clear, return fire, but subdue anyone surrendering. I doubted there'd be many with valuable information, other than those under the drill.

I kept Schaeffer aware as they moved closer to the cave opening. "Schaef, the one in the grey jacket is in charge. We need him."

"From the heavy fire they're laying down, I doubt this will end well." He'd sorted out his own assault team, our snipers providing backup as Schaeffer moved closer and closer to the drill.

The grey-coated man kept himself surrounded by his security people, but part of them had moved to the other side of the drill, where I'd seen the man earlier. They started to return our fire, covering him as he climbed up onto the drill. Our snipers took out several of the men, but he made it into the operator's box.

As he started to pull the drill from the hole, I saw the operator's intent. "Schaeffer, that's a laser drill. Get the men in the east quadrant out of there." I turned to the officer in charge of the second line. “We need to get him, at all costs.”

Freed from the rock face of the mountain, the laser started cutting a swath through the camp. The operator was shooting a slow broad band of laser fire, strong enough to cut through rock. He didn’t need to aim, simply sweep an area and destroy anything in the beam’s path.

“Everyone clear that quadrant, come around from the backside… wait!”

He shifted the laser upwards as he moved closer to the plateau. “He’s going for the shuttle! Team three, get that shuttle out of there, now!” I shouted the order, just as the skids lifted off the rock.

“They won’t shoot their own shuttle down.” My liaison officer tried to sound confident.

“Yes they will. This is a kill or be killed scenario.” I felt sick saying those words. Sicker as the weapon crested the cliff. “Get out of there!” I shouted over the comm, but nothing could stop what was happening as the laser grazed the port engine.

It exploded and the shuttle started spinning. Whoever was piloting fought the controls, but the spin brought it back into the beam, slashing into the fuselage. A second explosion in the damaged engine did what the pilot couldn’t, throwing the shuttle away from the ledge, out of range of the laser and into trees.

“Shuttle, report!” I was on my feet before my liaison could stop me.

The only ways to the plateau was the camp or the forest. Without the help of the Parredet, I couldn’t make it all the way around on my own, so I plunged down the steep path to the camp, ignoring the shouts of my liaison.

I ignored Schaeffer too, but not my training. I had my weapon charged and used it as I made my way across the rubble. The ramp to the plateau was on the other side of the drill. With the shuttle no longer a target, the laser was cutting down the cliff, rotating towards me. No, towards our second line.

Reaching Remy was my first priority, but duty kicked in. I slipped between tents and mining equipment, making my way to the drill.

Schaeffer wasn't yelling at me anymore. Crouched behind an ore crawler, I saw him between a rock crusher's tires. He signaled me to stay put, but that wasn't going to happen.

Signaling him back I got a scowl, then a nod. He passed a coded message to both teams. Between several deep breaths I studied my path, fixing it in my head, leaving my every reaction for the plan. Four…three…two… one! I burst out from my hiding spot and did a mad dash for the giant wheels of the drill.

Every weapon from our two teams was pointed at the drill or the other pods of resistance. Schaeffer's job was to keep their heads down and my path clear. My job was to take the drill operator out before his weapon reached the forest edge, team two, or any Parredet who lingered too close to the battlefield.

The path was in my head, a twisted variation of boot camp as I zigzagged twenty or so meters. The last thing I needed to pay attention to was the zip-zinging sounds of weapon fire aimed at me. Four meters, three… and my feet were off the ground, my hands out to grab a tire at least twice my height.

My toes scrambled for a hold, then rubber gripped rubber, my boots catching the wide treads. I scaled the tire, coming up at the side of the control chamber.

The operator didn't see me, his eyes focused on the ridge as my second line continued to fire at him. I grabbed at the door, jerked it open and swung my rifle up, opening fire with a laser blast that filled the control box.

The drill shut down abruptly. The chamber jerked to a stop as the operator's body fell onto the panel. Spinning around to jump to the ground, a fist landed on my jaw, knocking me back against the control chamber door. My head hit hard enough to make things go dark for a second, long enough for him to rip the rifle off my shoulder.

There was a blur of grey as my attacker yanked me to my feet, spinning me around as a body block for the snipers. "Okay, back off or we kill the pretty girl."

He shouted over my shoulder, making sure to move me around enough to keep anyone from taking a shot at him. I felt the metal of a pistol at my neck. I squeezed my eyes tight to drive away the fuzziness.

When I opened them Schaeffer stepped out from behind the rock crusher, his rifle pointed upwards. "Resisting is pointless. You don't have anywhere to go, especially since you destroyed your own shuttle."

The shuttle. That was why I was here. I had to get past the drill before I could get to the shuttle… no… to Remy. A voice shouted at me to think, to react. She was tearing to get out if I couldn't. I had to get to Remy.

No. I couldn't let her out. She wasn't trained for this. Kazan was. I was. The dizziness let go and my mind focused on what I had to do. I had to get away from this guy, then get up to the shuttle. I focused on Schaeffer as he closed the distance towards the driller. "Surrender and no one else has to get hurt."

"Surrender to who?"

"U.N. Space Alliance."

"Surrender to the Alliance? You don't have any authority here. This is outside Earth's solar system." The man in the grey jacket pulled the gun away from my throat to wave it at the mountain. "We claim this planet. This is our world."

"Yeah, see that's where we disagree, since this world is already occupied." Schaeffer pointed to the trees. "The residents are already pissed off."

"You mean the gorillas?" The camp leader laughed. "A few bananas ought to appease them. If not, they'll learn to stay away after we shoot a few of them out of their trees."

"Even if your assumptions were remotely true, you still can't claim this planet. We were here first. The Alliance. You and whoever you work for, have no rights here." Schaef pointed to his soldiers. "We intend to protect this world." His hand shifted to the sky. "We have two cruisers in orbit, way more of us than you."

The camp leader shook his head, shoving the pistol into my side. "We have a cruiser too, armed. You Alliance people never thought of that, did you? So it don't matter how many ships you got, once ours comes after you."

Schaeffer laughed. "You're misinformed. We didn't come to a gun fight with a knife. We're fully outfitted with weapons, so it's two against one, whenever your cruiser gets here. Which won't be for at least another month."

"We'll see. I can tell you my employers aren't going down without a fight. They're done with this Alliance monopoly." The gun dug deeper into my side. "I'm taking the girl and we're leaving." He pulled me backwards with him.

I had no idea how he intended to get us down from the tire, but I wasn't about to be a hostage. Until now I'd maintained the dazed affect, playing it now by letting my knees buckle and my body go limp.

He scrambled to pull me upright, not seeing my hand dig into my leg pocket. I came up fast, spinning around. He tried to grab at me again. A stunned expression replaced the anger. Face-to-face with him, I bared my teeth. "He might not have brought a knife, but I did." I jerked my blade free of his chest, flattening myself to the tire as his people started shooting at me.

Dropping down on the other side, I made a dash for cover as Schaeffer let go a barrage on the drill. Creeping around the huge machine, I saw the path to the plateau and ran. The way had been cut into rock, rubble plowed to the side of the ramp, providing me with cover. "Please be okay, please!"

I repeated the mantra with gasps by the time I crested the peak. I had to cover my face with my arm to keep from inhaling the acrid smoke spewing from the shuttle. "Remy!" I screamed his name, working around to the rear of the shuttle. "Remy!"

The tail end was open again, but the shuttle had landed on a boulder, nearly tipping the shuttle over onto its side. Someone had tried to lower the rear door, but I was on the wrong side to be able to look inside. There was no choice but to run back around the shuttle, through the toxic smoke.

My eyes burned from the fumes as I climbed through the opening. "Remy, where are you?" He didn't answer. No one did.

Backing out, I hacked out half a lung before being able to look around. Where was everyone? "Team Three, report!" My voice cracked as I shouted into my comm.

Schaeffer's voice responded in my ear. "What's the condition of the team?"

"They're gone. The shuttle's empty." I moved clear of it, searching the ground. There were a lot of footprints, but also blood. "There's injuries." Blood trailed towards the trees. "They must have gone into the forest for cover. Get up here as soon as it's clear."

I saw our sister shuttle appear over the trees, but there was no time to wait. I followed the trail into the trees, five meters, ten, deep enough the shuttles were barely visible, then the blood trail ended. No soldiers. Now real panic surged. “Remy, where are you?”

After screaming his name until my throat hurt, there was a rustling behind me. I turned to give orders to the soldiers Schaeffer sent after me. Instead a female Parredet dropped to the lowest branch, extending her arm to me. “Reee…meee.”

CHAPTER NINETEEN

My mind formed terrible images, fed by silence, fed by Batista's fear. She was terrified. So was I. Why didn't they answer? How bad were they injured? I hailed them several times and was near screaming when someone finally answered. "This is Ops Base. We got locals dropping in with wounded… confirmation, Team Three. We have Team Three."

"Ops Base, this is Col. Kazan. Give me a status. Who's wounded, how bad?"

"Colonel, you'll have to wait. We just got them and need to do triage before we can tell you anything." There was a pause. "We're aware your husband is part of the team. Give us a chance to stabilize the situation. Hold…"

"Shara, it's Lizzy. I'm here. I'll take care of Remy. The Parredet are going out again to get more wounded from the camp."

"Okay, Lizzy." Hearing her voice calmed me a little. "I should be there in a few minutes. Tell him I'm coming."

"Will do, gotta go!"

Lizzy terminated her end. The Parredet carrying me let out a strange sound, maybe trying to comfort me. Maybe because I was crying into her shoulder. I bit back the rest of my tears, holding my breath.

She moved gracefully, quickly, I heard the camp before seeing it, voices shouted out orders, engines fired up for departure. My friend swung down to lower branches. With a practiced grasp of my arm and twist of her body, she deposited me on the edge of the clearing.

I was already running to where at least a dozen soldiers were laid out on the ground, people hovering about them. For as tiny as she was, Lizzy was easy to find in the chaos. She knelt next to a man covered with an emergency blanket. It had to be Remy. I wove my way through the medics and support personnel, pushing someone out of my way.

Lizzy's eyes were dark when she looked up and saw me. She jumped to her feet and rushed for me. "Shara… I'm sorry… He's bad, real bad."

"Let go!" I jerked free of her hands and in a few more steps saw Remy. Burns covered his exposed head and shoulders, making him unrecognizable, but I knew it was him. I dropped to my knees. "Remy, I'm here."

His hand twitched. Gently I slipped my fingers into his and they tightened. He knew I was with him. "You're going to be alright. We just need to get you onboard." He didn't respond. "Remy, I promise."

He squeezed my hand again, but it wasn't a response. It was in pain. I could feel it radiating from him. "Medic! I need a medic over here."

Lizzy slipped up on Remy's other side, not holding back her tears. "Honey, they've already done all they can. He was just waiting for you."

"No! Don't say that. Medics!" I screamed, but they didn't even look up from their other patients. "Medics…"

"Shara, you only have a few more minutes…"

"Noooo…" I screamed at her, at Remy, at the sky. The spinning of the coin in my head was quick, landing with force on Batista. I clutched at Remy's hand. "You can't leave me! Don't leave. Fight!"

I was answered by keening from all around us, then a rush of Parredet. Yinet was with them, grabbing Lizzy and pulling her away from Remy, setting her aside and reaching for me.

More gently, but firmly, she peeled my hand from Remy's, pulling me to my feet and away as several males surrounded Remy. They removed the blanket. Only then could I see how burnt and broken his body was. It was horrible, but I couldn't look away.

Lizzy came to my side, her face turned to my shoulder. "What are they doing?"

"I don't know."

One of the males poured a liquid into Remy's mouth, tilting his head back so involuntary reactions made him swallow. One of our medics finally pushed up next to me. "What are they doing to him? He can't be handled."

I had no idea what was happening, but I sensed something in Remy relax. I looked at Yinet and she gave me a slow head bob. A nod. "It doesn't matter does it? You've already written him off for dead." I couldn't help sounding harsh. "If they can help him, I don't care what they do."

The medic didn't argue, or leave. He knelt down, watching as the males unwrapped large leaves, spreading them out on the ground like a blanket. Over those they laid down a second layer of a different leaf, broad, but filmy looking.

The trees above rustled again as another Parredet arrived. An old female. She joined the males, handing them flasks and chirping out orders. They started pouring a thick gel onto the top leaves, while she went to crouch over Remy.

Her cheek almost touched his lips. She gave a soft chirp and moved on down his body, speaking to the males as she pointed to the burns and breaks. The medic crept closer, giving the woman a nod as he grasping Remy's ankle. "Pulse is barely there, but it's steady, as if… as if they've suspended him?"

Lizzy turned her head off my shoulder, but looking at Yinet, not Remy. She made several gestures, pointing to Remy. "Deep sleep, no pain. He can't feel what they're doing." She knelt down to touch some of the gel spilled onto the bottom layer of leaves. "Hmmm, kind of feels like the… ow, ow, ow…"

She quickly wiped her fingers off on her pant leg. "Yeah, that's what they gave me for my feet, but a thousand times stronger…damn." She flicked her fingers. "Totally numb, like they've been cut off."

"Really?" The medic reached to sample it for himself, but the old woman made a clucking noise at him. "Okay. Guess I better not." He looked at the bed of gel and at Remy. "They're going to wrap him up in that stuff. It heals?"

"The diluted stuff did for me, real quick too." Lizzy asked Yinet, their talking accompanied by hand signals. Their hands flew through motions, Lizzy giving the briefest of interpretations, busy jumping to the next question in her head.

Finally she nodded and looked at the old woman still looking over Remy. "Yeah. They're going to wrap him up, but mostly keep him in a coma type state, since it's the pain that is stealing his soul… ability to fight. Then you can do whatever repairs you have to."

The medic nodded. "Okay, I get most of that. Can I help? I know human anatomy better than they do. We need to work something out to deliver medications and oxygen. His lungs are burned by the toxic fumes. And I need to realign his broken bones, as best as possible."

He spoke to Lizzy, but did his best to mimic what he wanted, what was wrong internally with Remy. The old woman was watching him, listening as Yinet translated what both he and Lizzy were saying. She waved a hand over Remy, stopping where bones erupted through his thigh. She gave a twist of her hand, pointing to the medic.

"She says yes, put the bones where they belong." Lizzy tipped her head. "His clothes need to be removed."

"Yeah, we didn't get them all in triage." The medic pulled out a pair of surgical scissors and started cutting at the burned rags, having to peel singed fabric out of wounds." He barely glanced over his shoulder. "Kev, need you over here."

Lizzy wrapped her hand over my arm. "How you doing?"

"Can't answer that, but as long as he's still alive..." I wrapped my fingers in hers. "As long as I get him back. I have to get him back. She never wanted this… I never…"

"I know, honey. No one could have seen this happening." Lizzy wrapped her arms around me. "Just hang in there. Yinet won't let him die."

The other medic crept into the circle, frowning. "What are you doing, Jonas? He's a red tag. We have other wounded coming in right now."

Jonas looked over his shoulder and shook his head. "Kev, you're standing next to Mrs. Batista… Sorry about that, ma'am." He jerked his head at Kev. "Get your ass over here."

Kev bowed his head to me as he went to Jonas' side. "What are we doing?" He pulled out his own scissors and started removing cloth and flesh from Remy's other leg.

"The woman here is their doctor. We're getting Mr. Batista ready for some type of medical stasis. They already got him in a near coma." He jerked his head over to the leaves, the males meticulously adding more layers of gel. "We're going to learn some native medicine."

Kev looked over at the Parredet. "Okay, if you say so." He finished with the few strips left on Remy's leg.

CHAPTER TWENTY

Jonas checked Remy's pulse for the tenth time. "Go get me the LO kit. We'll fill up his lungs. That will keep his blood oxygenated… oh, and a tissue extraction kit."

"You'll explain more when I get back?" Kev was already getting up.

"Yeah, hurry. He still has a pulse, but I'm seeing more hypoxia." The old woman gave him a curious look. He pointed to his own lips, taking in a deep breath, then to Remy's as he mimicked trouble breathing.

"Wow, you're good at that." Lizzy sounded a bit jealous.

"Had to learn when I was a kid." He moved to kneel over Remy's head, tipping his head back as Kev returned.

Kev ripped open an intubation kit, leaning over with the tube while Jonas kept the airway open. "There's a lot of damage, but whatever they gave him seems to… yeah…"

He shifted his eyes away from Remy to a computer screen in the kit's lid. "Lots of damage, but the cords are relaxed. Going for the right lung first."

I didn't want to look, but had to, watching the inside of Remy's airway through a camera on the end of the tube. It should have been pink and red, but there were black smudges and blisters. In some places it looked like the tube couldn't get through, but it did.

Through the tube he inserted two smaller tubes, passing down until they appeared in the camera. The thinner one he worked deeper into the lung, the other he left near the camera.

"Okay, we can administer the LO." He reached over to the kit and activated the process. A blue fluid flowed through one of the tubes and into Remy.

It only took a minute before bubbles started flowing back up the airway. Kev activated the other tube and they were sucked into the tube. The color got darker, brackish. "Yeah, that's definitely not good. I'm upping saturation."

Jonas looked at me. "We're replacing the fluids already built up in his lungs with liquid oxygen. That will keep his blood oxygenated. We can also start delivering medication internally, try to keep infections from setting in."

His hands moved, explaining as best as possible the technology to the Parredet doctor." He saw Lizzy watching his hands. "My little brother was born with a defect to his auditory systems. For eight years it was the only way to talk to him. Guess you never forget it."

Lizzy nodded. "Babies learn sign language easier than standard languages, some signs coming naturally, like wanting food."

"Comes in handy." He looked at Remy, then to the old woman, tapping his lower lip. "Already working. Going pink again."

She gave him something of a smile, turning to the males as they finished their task. She rattled off something to them and they backed away from the leaves. From another bundle of leaves they started wrapping their hands.

Jonas watched them, leaving Kev to move on to Remy's left lung. He gave an odd smile as one finished and held his mittened paws up like some surgeon afraid to touch anything. "Every instinct is screaming for an anti-bacterial, but clearly we don't really have any choice right now. No offense..." His bobbed his head at me. "Not trying to be insensitive."

"No offense taken." I clung to Lizzy's hand, since she wasn't needed for translating at the moment. "I know the alternative. Is he ready to move?"

"Another minute. We just have to finish flushing out his other lung and hook up a pacemaker, just in case." Jonas got up, walking around Kev to pick up a smaller box. "I'm going to take a sample of muscle tissues. I suspect Mr. Batista will need some tissue transplants where the burns went too deep."

He moved to Remy's hip. "Going to take a little bone too, just in case. We can grow matching tissues he'll be less likely to reject."

He looked up at me. "Even if all this works, he's going to have a long hard recovery ahead of him." He cleaned off a patch of unburned skin between his hip and thigh. "You might not want to watch."

I couldn't imagine anything worse than how Remy looked right now. Burns covered most of his body and broken bones were visible where flesh was completely burned away. "Do it."

Remy might not have felt the extraction, but I jerked as Jonas bored into hip bone to get his samples.

Kev finished injected LO into Remy's lungs, the backflow coming out clearer. He was already feeding wires into Remy's chest, the computer guiding his positioning of them against heart muscle.

Jonas moved out of the way, coming to stand with me while Kev stayed with the LO unit. The Parredet converged on Remy, listening to the old woman, paying close attention to the fractures.

With their hands wrapped in leaves, they lifted Remy from the bloody surgical blanket. Supporting his broken limbs, they carried him to the bed of leaves and gel, laying him down gently.

Kev kept pace with them, keeping the breathing tubes from pulling loose.

They positioned him and the old woman waved Jonas to join her. He turned to me. "I know you think you have to be brave and all, but this is where we try to put his bones back where they belong. Please, step away for a moment. Please."

"Come on, Shara. Check in with Schaeffer." She pulled and I followed. Yinet came with us too, but didn't try to talk.

We looked around the clearing packed by patients with a variety of burns and wounds, from the shuttle crash or the shootout.

To the side of the clearing were four shapes, covered with emergency blankets. I knew they were bodies of soldiers. To another side of the clearing were wounded miners, our soldiers guarding them.

"What are we going to do with them?" It was a strange questions to come out of my mouth, Kazan not sharing anything with me right now.

The soldier nearest us shifted to look at me. He looked a bit confused by my question, that it came from me when I'd ordered them to fire at will. "They'll be transferred into our cargo hold, set up as a temporary brig. We'll bag the dead and send notifications to whatever family we identify. See what they want to done with them."

"Like send them the bodies?" Lizzy sounded somewhat appalled. "They're criminals."

"The ashes, unless it violates religious practices."

"Pretty damn sure they wouldn't return the courtesy if it was us." Lizzy snipped at him, looking at the bodies on our side of the clearing. "No one would know what happened to us."

"True, ma'am, but that difference makes us the good guys"

Lizzy bit at her lip, looking back to where Remy lay in the care of aliens. "Guess so."

Right now I didn't care what side we were on. I wanted to be with Remy.

When we finally got to return to Remy the men were wrapping his body. Kev and Jonas helped, their hands in multiple layers of gloves. They smoothed gel-drenched leaves around Remy's limbs, looking a lot like the Egyptian mummy process. The old woman worked on his face, being careful of the tubes.

"What happens when this part is done?"

Jonas got up, leaving Kev to learn this bizarre medicine. "We'll further stabilize his breaks, then move him up to the ship. As I understand the process, we have to keep the wraps saturated."

He looked back at the old woman. "She agrees to come up with us to manage his care. If we can get him through the next few days and his stats come up, he stands a chance."

"I have to go with him." I looked between Lizzy and Yinet, suddenly feeling defensive, waiting for Kazan to pop up and say I couldn't go. "I have to go."

"Yes, Shara, you do." Lizzy signed to Yinet, then wrapped her arms around me. "Schaef can deal with the rest of this. You go with Remy."

I squeezed Lizzy in my arms and almost broke down completely when I felt Yinet's cheek against mine. I fought off the tears, but didn't let go of my two friends until the medics started to carry Remy to the waiting shuttle.

I traded their embraces for Remy's fingers, the only part of him I could cling to.

CHAPTER TWENTY-ONE

The old Parredet doctor came with us, chattering and signing with Jonas. Apparently gender taboos didn't apply to doctors. Zemor introduced herself to the entire medical staff once aboard the ship, then joined me as they put Remy into an isolation room.

For three days I sat with him, except for the few times they made me leave while they did surgeries to repair internal bleeds. I slept on a cot next to him and talked to him about anything, everything.

Jonas encouraged it, saying the tests proved Remy had no brain injuries and was lucid, even in this coma state. The gel and drug Zemor gave him only blocked the transmission of pain signals from his body to his brain.

She willingly gave Jonas samples of all the medications she was using on Remy. From our quiet cubicle, I watched as Jonas improvised using them on other patients, substituting the porous webbed leaves with medical gauze. Zemor supervised, teaching Parredet medicine to the entire medical staff.

I sat and talked, and waited. This was day three, the day Jonas promised they'd reevaluate Remy's condition. Zemor had already withheld the drug keeping him in such a deep state, but it would take a while to work out of his system.

The tubes still ran into his lungs, but the brackish bloody fluid had stopped. The fluid was returning almost clear, meaning the LO was being absorbed. That gave me as much hope as his brain waves responding when I spoke.

I kept talking. "Schaef gave me an update. The miners' information led to the company financing this. The Alliance seized it and arrested all the executives. They got the location where they've been taking the ore and are setting up barricades. He says that we're going to take advantage of what they put into play. If we can make a deal with the Parredet for setting up our own mining process, we'll be that much further ahead."

I didn't expect a reaction, not yet. "Schaef said he's going to sponsor bringing you aboard. If we start building more ships, we're going to need more engineers. We can finally work together, if that's what you want."

His fingers were warm and I laid my face against them. "Or we can settle in one place and start that family we always talked about."

A few of the tears I'd been holding at bay since we got here slipped out, but only a few. I hadn't let myself really cry. I was afraid if I let go of my tears, I'd be letting go of hope. I'd be letting go of him. "I really want a family, Remy. I want it with you."

More tears threatened to slip out, so I squeezed my eyes tight. "So, you just got to come out of this. I need you." I clung to his hand, clinging to the image of children. Our children. I'd go anywhere he wanted. I'd wait for as long as it took.

I brushed my cheek across his fingers, until one rose up slightly to brush against my ear. I froze, wondering if I'd imagined it, but a second later his finger moved again. I kept his hand to my face. "Remy, are you waking up? Please wake up, if just for a minute."

His finger moved and he made a sound, garbled because of the tubes. "Oh my God." I pressed his hand to my face harder. "I'm right here. Don't try to move, or talk. They have tubes in your lungs, so you can… breathe. Let me call them in here." His fingers answered, closing around my hand.

"Medic Jonas, I yelled his name at the computer board over the bed. "Jonas, get in here!" I could see him raise his head from another patient. He spoke to Zemor and they both headed our direction. "They're coming in, Remy. Just hang on."

Both burst into the room, other medical staff starting to converge on the cubicle walls. "He's waking up?" Jonas went to the computer board, looking at the brain scans. "He's conscious. That's…" Zemor chattered something, not sounding surprised, only confident. Jonas laughed slightly. "Of course he is."

He leaned over Remy. "Mr. Batista. Glad to have you back. You can't talk right now. Tap Shara's hand, once for yes, twice for no. Understand."

His finger moved, once. "Yes." I responded, even though everyone could see.

"Great. Do you know what happened?"

"Yes."

"You were critically injured when the shuttle crashed."

"Yes."

"The Parredet have been treating you with their medicines. You've been in a sedated state and we have your body wrapped in an analgesic gel."

"Yes." I rested my lips to his hand. I'd told him everything that happened, hoping he'd hear and wouldn't panic when he woke up. He heard me.

Jonas asked a few more questions, assessing awareness and pain. Satisfied he looked to me. "This part might be a bit difficult for both of you. I'm going to start reducing the LO mixture, replacing it with real oxygen. If your lungs start to spasm, that's a good sign. don't fight it. They'll be wanting to expand on their own."

"Yes." He tapped once, then gripped my hand. "He's ready."

Zemor came around the bed to my side as Jonas started reducing the liquid oxygen, replacing it with the real thing. Fluid continued to be suctioned from his lungs as one replaced the other.

It took a few minutes, but his hand around mine tightened. "Okay baby, remember what Jonas said. Let it happen." I looked across to Jonas, seeing him removing the LO tubes completely. Panic ran through me, wondering if it was too soon, if Remy's lungs were ready. Out came the suction tubes, then the large intubation tube.

Remy gagged, coughed and fought to breathe, his hand clutched at mine. My panic had me squeezing back, but Jonas was pressing a hand to Remy's chest. "Inhale. Come on. You have to do this part on your own. You want to see your wife's face? Breathe!"

"Remy, breathe. Come on!"

The gasps coming from him sounded agonizing, but his chest rose and fell, then rose again, and again, each time with less panic.

Zemor sounded pleased, waving her hand at Remy's body, but then flicked her hand when she reached Remy's head.

"Yes. Let's let him see Mrs. Batista." Jonas looked at me, still clinging to Remy. "Keep in mind his condition. Don't expect too many miracles. From here out we're facing a whole new set of challenges."

"I understand." Remy squeezed my hand. "So does he."

CHAPTER TWENTY-TWO

"How's it working?" I watched Remy pace across the room, slowly turn and walk back.

He looked up, smiling. "Much better. Told you it would only take a few tweeks." He stopped, raising his leg and flexing the knee. "A lot more stable."

"Well, once the bone grafts are set you won't need those braces anymore, though I'll take you any way I can."

Remy took the last few steps to reach where I sat on the edge of my desk. He leaned over me, pulling my hips to his. "How about right here?"

I laughed, wrapping my arms around his neck. Scars still zigged and zagged on his cheek and down one side of his neck, disappearing into his shirt. New patches of skin still settling in. I really didn't care. He was alive and we were back, if only for a visit. "Yinet and Gerret will be howling for us to join them any minute. We've been gone forever."

"Well, they'll just have to wait a little longer." He kissed me, leaning me backwards over the desk as his hands fumbled with my jeans.

"Remy!" I laughed, trying to push his hands away. "You're being crazy. We have to go."

"Not yet." His hands grabbed mine, pinning them down on the desk. "A deal's a deal. We're going to start that family we're always talking about."

"Right this second?" I squirmed, which didn't help. Neither did his teeth behind my ear.

"Right this second…" He let go of one hand, reaching for the zipper of my jeans again.

He was winning this argument, until the door opened. "Oh, geez. Remy, put your pants on!" Lizzy giggled, slamming the hut door and yelling through it. "Learn to use the lock."

"Killjoy." He turned his back and reached for his jeans as she opened the door again.

"It's not dead, just deflated a bit." She grinned at me.

I scurried to tuck my shirt back in, glaring back at Lizzy. "You could learn to knock."

"Yeah, I could." She smirked. "Glad to see you still have all the working parts, Remy."

"Another minute you'd have gotten the full show." He had his pants on and turned back around. "We heard congratulations are in order. Schaeffer tamed you."

"I wouldn't go that far." Lizzy rolled her eyes away from both of us. "I just thought that I could pitch a more permanent tent here."

"Well, permanent remains to be seen. No matter what Yinet might like, our staying on here, in any capacity, has to be approved by all the clans." I grabbed both our coats, while Remy pulled his boots on.

"Well, that's why I came here, I think. Yinet wants to take us somewhere. I think it's a meeting with the clan mothers, though she's not explaining it as thoroughly as usual. She's using words our translator program doesn't know yet."

"Well, now you have my attention." I gave Remy a smile as he grunted. "Sorry, babe. I promise to let you have your way with me later."

"Yeah, promises." He put on his coat and went to the bags, packed in case our first outing ran late and we had to spend the night with the Parredet.

I started to go help him, but resisted. He insisted on doing everything he could, but agreed to ask for help when he got tired. He gave me a wink as he pulled his own pack on, then handed me my own. "Lead on, Lizzy."

"Zip up. It's full on winter." She pulled her hood up and threw the door open again. Thankfully it wasn't a straight blast of cold air. Small windbreak tents had been constructed onto the front of the hard tents, as a buffer for the real cold and to knock off snow.

I stayed beside Remy as Lizzy led us towards the shuttle landing pad. Our first exposure to the elements had played havoc with his braces. He'd spent our first hour here reinsulating the electronic leads. Now we'd really find out how good a job he did fixing them.

We reach the shuttle without a breakdown and he made it up the ramp on his own. We squeezed through another buffer screen and into the shuttle. I brought up the rear, stepping through last and into a hug from Yinet. Remy got a similar treatment from Gerret, just not as vigorous. They'd been warned he was still recovering.

I mumbled through the coat and bear hug, until Yinet put me down again. "Yeah, glad to be back too. Didn't expect to see you here."

"I told you they wanted to take us somewhere." Lizzy rolled her eyes and went forward to where Schaeffer sat waiting to take off, getting to slide into the co-pilot seat. "We're ready. Crank up the heat and let's go."

"Yes, ma'am." Schaeffer started closing the hatch. "She's gotten real bossy around here while you were gone. Worse than you were."

"Bite me, Dick. You know how it works." She leaned over her chair as he extended his cheek, giving him a nuzzle. "You might be sheriff, but I'm substitute Clan Mom around these here parts."

"Clan Mom?" Remy asked.

"Substitute?" I spoke at the same time.

Lizzy swung her chair around as we got buckled in, Yinet and Gerret settling into a bench with improvised safety straps. "Yeah, someone had to slide into the role when you left. That was the problem before, besides liking you, there wasn't a female clan leader for them. By their standards and your behavior, you were clan mother, like Yinet. Right?"

"Yezzz. You arrre Clan Mother." Yinet responded with her version of a smile.

"Wow, your standard is really coming along." I darted glances between her and Lizzy. "Very impressed."

"Well, there's still words our programs can't identify, but it's only been a year." Lizzy stopped as Schaeffer lifted the shuttle off the ground. She waited until he set course and relaxed. "Want to bring up the holo-map, show us where we're going?"

"See, bossy." Schaeffer tapped up the computer's hologram program and set it to project in the space between our seats. He turned his chair around partway, not totally relinquishing control of the shuttle to the computer. "Gerret identified an area they want us to see, though he didn't tell me why." He gave Gerret a half shrug. "All will be revealed soon enough."

I leaned forward, studying the coordinates mapped. "This is where we're going?"

"No, I just thought it was pretty." Lizzy rolled her eyes at me again. "Geez, get your head on straight."

"Wow, Schaef, did you really propose or she just tell you you're getting married and you're too scared to say no?" Remy pointed to his legs when Lizzy looked like she was going to come after him with a kick to the shins.

Schaeffer laughed. "So, this is where we're going. Our preliminary scans ruled it out, mostly because we couldn't get a good reading. The terrain was too rough to set up a camp."

"So, what do we know now? We've been here for over two years." I looked over to Yinet. "What's so important there?"

Yinet didn't answer me, but Gerret leaned forward. He tapped areas around the map and I recognized their community, then others. He kept marking other locations and it took a minute or two for me to realize none were within the zone. I couldn't see why, it looked just as untamed as the rest of their world. Tall mountains with a few pastoral valleys and forest from rim to rim.

"You're taking us someplace you don't go. Is it safe?"

"No danger." Yinet turned her face away from the map, starring out her window. "Wait."

I gave Schaeffer a look and after a year he still understood it, shutting down the display. Yinet wasn't angry, but looking at the map upset her.

Lizzy gave me a subtle nod, agreeing this had to be dropped for now. She was quick to fill the awkward silence. "Now that you're back we can start planning this wedding." Schaeffer groaned and turned back to the cockpit. "Shut up!" She snipped at him. "He doesn't see why we have to do this."

"He's a guy."

"No, it's not that." He grumbled from the cockpit, not turning around. "You keep talking about family. Part of why we were picked for this mission is that we had no family."

"Well, you made a family. You've been living with most of these people for years, sharing secrets, sharing experiences. That's what makes families and they want to share this." She swung her chair back to me. "Besides, it's not all about you."

"Schaef, buddy." Remy stroked my arm. "Once these sisters get their hearts set on something, they team up."

"Like I haven't figured that out?"

"Then stop fighting it. Rank has no privileges here. The only answer is 'yes, dear, whatever you want'. I heard Gerret snicker and Remy looked over to see his friend nod. "See, it's a universal rule."

"So, back to the wedding." I couldn't resist. "I know you put it off to spring."

"Well, I had to wait until the two of you got back. And it's too cold right now. I want someplace special, either the rock or the plaza." That got Yinet's attention. Lizzy sat a little straighter, opening up her computer and sending a picture of the plaza to the hologram. "The rock is where we all met, but your home is where we really came together. And it's so beautiful in the spring."

A few taps and the image advanced to show the rapid blooming of flowers around the edges of the plaza and the few places vines were allowed to climb the face of the cliffs.

"Oh, that is so pretty. I can see a wedding there." I'd missed the entire year and had no clue what spring in the mountains looked like. "As long as no one minds a bunch of humans showing up."

"We are honored. Human and Parredet together."

"There, that was easy." I knew Lizzy wouldn't use her wedding as a diplomatic ploy, but the thought crossed my mind. "Maybe there's some Parredet customs you can incorporate."

"Maybe…" I could see Lizzy's creative side kicking in. "Yinet, we're going to have to sit down and exchange stories." She leaned back to look at Schaeffer, grinning. "Maybe you better have a chat with Gerret so you don't get any weird surprises."

"Yes, dear… whatever… you… want." Gerret snickered again, strangely wicked enough to make Schaeffer look back. "I have a feeling I'm not going to like this."

"Hey, you only get married once." I gave Schaeffer a wink. "Till death do you part."

"Like even that matters." Remy tapped his chest. "I'm still here."

CHAPTER TWENTY-THREE

It took nearly two hours for us to reach the coordinates, Gerret pointing Schaeffer to fly around the zone and land on the southern rim of a particular string of mountains. As we dropped altitude we saw other Parredet, waving us towards a clearing.

I could see Schaeffer squinting to survey the ground, but they'd done a good job smoothing it out for us. He settled down in the center. Snow flurried up around us, but fluttered down again quickly. Yinet unbuckled and gathered up winter gear from the bench behind her.

While we had spent almost a year on the planet before finally communicating with the Parredet, they never showed themselves during the worst three months.

We'd originally assumed the Parredet went into some type of hibernation. Now we knew they just hunkered down, since any travel had to be by foot. She pulled on hide boots and a heavy fur coat. Gerret joining her.

"I take it we're going for a hike?" I looked to Remy. "Will the terrain be difficult?"

Yinet pulled her hood up, only her eyes showing as she tightened it around her face. "No. Gerret will lead Remy."

“I’ll be fine.” Remy pulled on his parka. “The braces work now.” He tossed me my parka. “Let’s go see what’s here.”

Despite their bickering, Schaeffer was bundling up Lizzy, making sure everything was tucked in for the cold. He snuck a kiss before pulling the strings around her hood. It was odd to see how he’d gotten used to the displays of affection. “I’ll be with Gerret and Remy.”

I almost laughed as Lizzy waddled towards us. Though Schaeffer found gear her size, she was just too tiny under all the insulation. She mumbled something, following Yinet to the wind buffer at the rear of the shuttle. We all fell in behind Lizzy, stepping out into the cold and snow.

Tramping through the drift reminded me of Colorado, except for the sasquatch-shaped Parredet closing in on our group.

Yinet led us out of the clearing and onto a path cut through the trees. Curiosity was killing me as to where they were taking us, but I already knew not to keep asking. The Parredet couldn’t be rushed into anything. Besides, they couldn’t be taking us far.

I told myself that as my toes started going numb. I glanced back to check on Remy, knowing he couldn’t tolerate the cold, regardless of thermal enhanced braces.

Yinet caught me, pointing ahead of us where the path led through two massive boulders. “Not far.” Two Parredet moved around us, running up the last twenty meters. “They will prepare for Remy.”

“Thank you. He still needs time to heal. It will be a difficult winter, but we both felt we had to come back.” I glanced at him again. “Part of the healing process.”

Yinet’s upper body seemed to nod, urging me to keep going.

We finished the last few meters in silence, reaching the crest of the path, only to find it ran downhill from here. My first thought was to protest, for Remy, but Yinet didn't even look in that direction, instead turning onto a side path that wrapped around one of the boulders, dropping to broad steps. I caught up. Turning another corner, there was the entrance to a cave.

Lizzy and I stopped to look at the face of the cliff, seeing none of the carvings that told their story. Yinet beckoned us into the cave as the males descended the steps. We entered, grateful to find a warm chamber behind a heavy woven curtain. I recognized Parredet Clan Mothers already gathered around a crackling fire.

Unprepared for this meeting, I stalled, waiting for Remy, walking with him to the roaring fire, helping him strip off the heavy boots and coat. A young Parredet offered Remy a blanket and took our gear back to hang at the door.

Remy already saw the protocol and took a seat at the second ring, first ring for the females. Probably just as well, he was as sensitive to heat as he was cold. In true Parredet fashion, no one spoke until all the males joined their mates. Until everyone was seated.

Lizzy took a spot between me and Yinet, a habit even before I left. Funny, before I'd had twinges of jealousy about their relationship. The year off had certainly helped me integrate my personalities into one. I even took my married name, Col. Shara Batista now. I turned to look at Remy and he smiled, letting me know he was fine, to stop doting.

I was drawn back to the circle when a song started, a ritual before the Clan Mothers started their meetings. It was their way of turning off everything except the purpose of the meeting, though I had yet to hear of any conflicts in the Parredet. We had a lot to learn from them about maintaining peace.

We sat quietly through the song, curious, but anxious as I looked at the faces of the Parredet. They all looked serious, solemn. Had we done something wrong? The song ended and that anxiety rose as all eyes shifted to me.

Yinet broke the awkward silence, nudging Lizzy. “You bring the book?”

“Always.” Lizzy reached into the pack tucked between her feet, pulling out her artist pad, digging for an art pencil until Yinet gently took the pad from her.

Yinet flipped to the early pages. “In another age, we lived different. We lived to hold, to take. We paid for greed.” She held up the page Lizzy had drawn from the caves, depicting their ancient city.

The group was quiet, bowing their heads. “We fled terror.” She flipped to another page. “Our home.” The picture showed the exodus of her people from a city crushed by war. “To find our…vetra.” She tapped at her chest.

“Souls.” Lizzy whispered to us.

Silently, looking at the drawing, I felt a similarity to stories of our religious past, to the exodus of Gomorrah where a few fled their homes to save themselves from God’s vengeance.

“We fled. Build future free of war. Never return to downfall.” She pointed to the city, then circled the valley it encompassed.

As she told us this, Gerret translated to those Parredet who didn’t understand our language. Many of the Clan Mothers nodded, barely glancing at the art work.

Yinet lowered the pictures, staring at me. “Your people are young. You follow path of danger. For rock.” She pulled a lump of the ore from her pocket. “Enemy follow you.”

"We won't bring them back." I looked to Schaeffer, getting a nod. "We found those responsible and seized their operations."

"People leave, new people arrive. In time, people die."

I knew she implied the future we had no control over and I dropped my eyes. "No, I can't give absolute guarantees. I can only hope, as time goes by, that those in power uphold the laws we have in place now."

I glanced to Schaeffer again. "We came here looking for the ore, but now that we've proven this world isn't open to us, we'll have to leave. We'll keep looking."

"If you do not leave?"

I looked up at her. "We have no choice. This is your world. At most, with your permission, we can maintain communications and learn more from each other."

A murmur passed around the gathering when Gerret translated my words. Yinet hushed them, her eyes focusing on me harder. "You hunt ore." She raised her hand to imply space.

She lifted the picture of the valley. "You find ore here. We never go here. You live here. Learn here. Learn danger of vetra going too far. Parredet protect vetra of friend, human."

I looked at her, then at the faces of the other Clan Mothers. "Are you offering us this land, to stay here?" No one reacted, except my own people, heads turning to look at each other in as much confusion as I felt. "You're going to allow the Alliance to colonize and mine the ore?"

"Under condition." Yinet bowed to the other Parredet. "We make pact." She pointed to me, then lifted the pad of paper, showing the valley, pointing to the entrance of the cave. "All land here to Clan Mother Ara."

"Clan Mother Ara?" Lizzy snickered. "Now it's your turn."

Schaeffer reached for his backpack. “We need to properly document this. We’ll need to set up a scan record of the area so we can map out the exact area being offered.” He tapped at his comm, then scowled. “Can’t get a signal in here.”

“Excuse me.” I stood up before he could. Yinet tilted her head, confused. “This is more than I imagined. I’m… overwhelmed. Let me have a moment to process this.”

Lizzy did a quick short interpretation, getting a sympathetic nod. “Schaef, I’ll call the ship and have them send the most recent scans.” My heart was pounding out of my chest, trying to process what had just happened. “Give me a few minutes.”

He frowned, but nodded, giving me a squint. I could imagine his voice in my head, telling me to get my act together before I blew the deal.

“Thank you. I’ll just be a few minutes. Lizzy, get a few more details for me?”

“Sure, hon. Get your scans.” She gave me the same warning look, then turned to Yinet again to repeat the offer just made.

I tried to block it out as I bowed to the Clan Mothers, grabbed my coat and made a dash out the entrance. I gasped from the burst of cold and the anxiety hitting at the same time.

The wall of the cliff supported me as I bent over, taking deep breathes so I didn’t pass out. It took a minute to calm down enough to contact the ship, ordering the scans for the surrounding coordinates.

While I downloaded the scans, I looked out over the valley. I couldn’t see the other rim because of clouds, but this had to be hundreds of miles of territory. They were giving this to us… no, giving it to me. Naming me Clan Mother.

"You alright, babe?" Remy stepped up beside me.

"No, I'm freaking out. They can't do this."

"What, make a pact with humans?" He huddled up in his coat.

"No, with me. It's all hanging on me. I'm just a colonel, a cog in a huge wheel. I can't represent all humans in this." I clasped my head, sure if anything would bring Kazan back full force, this would do it. "I can't accept. I can't do that to you. I made you a promise. I almost lost you once before. I won't let that happen again."

"You won't." Remy's hands covered mine, pulling them away from my temples, replacing them with his own. "Take a breath and calm down. We're in this together, remember, Col. Batista? This is what you came here to do."

He made me look at him, which didn't help, his scars a reminder of what my secrets almost cost us both. "I made you a promise."

"Which you haven't broken. What is really scaring you? Focus."

I did, pulling on everything I knew, everything Kazan knew, sorting out what I'd just heard. "What if we make a mistake? This is why we were looking for worlds without sentient life. What if we want to go home? What about having kids? And that doesn't even take into account how the Alliance is going to take this. Colonization of an inhabited world? Me being the condition this all hangs on? Me in charge of a whole planet? That would drive them crazy."

"Whoa there, slow down, take another breath before you explode." Remy grinned, unclutching my face to tuck his hands back inside his coat.

"I don't know which of those to respond to first. Hmmm… Let's go with the Alliance. They want the ore. It could take years, centuries or never to find this stuff again. They'll agree to the terms of the pact."

"Yeah, I guess." That made sense. "But I'm one of the terms."

"Okay, so what? You've been in charge for a long time and you're good at it. So cross that off the list." He unfolded his arms long enough to make a slashing gesture.

"It's more than being 'in charge', I'm one of the terms. I'd be Clan Mother."

"So? It's not like we're taking over the whole planet. It'll be a small colony. You've been doing it for years."

"I'm one of the terms." I kept repeating myself, repeating Yinet. "Staying here is not in our plans."

"Ahhh, now we get back to me, and what I want." Remy stepped up close, all but wrapping his arms around me.

"Consider this. Our kids would be the first generation to grow up here, knowing humans aren't alone in the galaxy, or the universe. They'd grow up living among Parredet. They'd be a whole new generation of humans. What more could I ask for them?"

"You're an engineer. You wanted to build the next generation of ships."

Remy shook his head. "I've never tried to fool myself into believing I'd ever be able to return to full duty. I'm not going to start now."

He let out a long sigh, as if giving up something he had been holding onto. Something he didn't want anymore. "If given the choice between being given some patronizing job reviewing ship designs, or staying here and building something real with you and our children, there's no contest. I want this. I want us to stay here."

"Really?" I huddled up against him. "All I want is you, over everything else, even this. If you want to stay here, then I do too."

I turned my head, laying it on his chest as I looked out over the massive range. “So, it’s going to be a strange new challenge for all of us.”

“Yes. The 23rd century is going to bring us all new lives.”

“And a new Alliance.” I looked up at the winter sun. “The Interstellar Alliance.”

18384223R00085

Made in the USA
San Bernardino, CA
12 January 2015